D0445165

Hello from
RENN
LAKE

Also by Michele Weber Hurwitz

Calli Be Gold

The Summer I Saved the World . . . in 65 Days

MICHELE WEBER HURWITZ

 Published in the United States by Wendy Lamb Books, an imprint of Random House Children's Books, a division of Penguin Random House LLC, New York.

Wendy Lamb Books and the colophon are trademarks of Penguin Random House LLC.

Visit us on the Web! rhcbooks.com

Educators and librarians, for a variety of teaching tools, visit us at RHTeachersLibrarians.com

Library of Congress Cataloging-in-Publication Data
Names: Hurwitz, Michele Weber, author.
Title: Hello from Renn Lake / Michele Weber Hurwitz.
Description: First edition. | New York: Wendy Lamb Books, [2020] | Includes bibliographical references. | Summary: In Wisconsin, as her adoptive parents open their Renn Lake cabins for summer visitors, twelve-year-old Annalise, abandoned as an infant and protected by the lake, discovers a growing toxic algae bloom and teams up with her friends to save Renn Lake.
Identifiers: LCCN 2019023241 (print) | LCCN 2019023242 (ebook) | ISBN 978-1-9848-9632-2 (hardcover) | ISBN 978-1-9848-9633-9 (library binding) | ISBN 978-1-9848-9634-6 (ebook)
Subjects: CYAC: Lakes—Fiction. | Water—Pollution—Fiction. | Environmental protection—Fiction. | Abandoned children—Fiction. | Adoption—Fiction.
Classification: LCC PZ7.H95744 He 2020 (print) | LCC PZ7.H95744 (ebook) | DDC [Fic]—dc23

The text of this book is set in 12-point Chronicle.
Interior design by Ken Crossland

Printed in the United States of America
10 9 8 7 6 5 4 3 2 1
First Edition

To Lake Geneva: I fondly remember our many summers together ♥

Before

RENN

There are two beginnings of this story: mine, which goes back further than you can imagine, and the girl's, which goes back only twelve years. From the day I first saw her in the bassinet, I knew we would be forever connected. The day she was left here.

First, my beginning. When the glaciers were melting, ice and water shaped the land. My cousin Tru came before me, long curves of gray and green, and miles of muddy brown. As the ice carved jagged bluffs and a large, deep basin, I filled up with rain and snowmelt. Pine and linden trees sprouted around my shores, and the sun began to warm me.

After much time passed, people arrived and settled nearby. People like to name things; they called us Nepew, the Menominee word for water. I gave them a place to cool off, to bathe and drink. Fish were plentiful. The trees had grown tall, and shade was abundant.

Then other people came, wearing different clothing, speaking different languages, and things changed. There was fighting, blood spilled on my shore, and many died. I watched, silent and uneasy, unable to help. Afterward, nothing was the same.

The other people, explorers, gave us new names. The tallest among them, a man wearing a fur coat, called me Renn, after the place he came from, Rennar. It sounded strange after being called Nepew for so long. He named my cousin Troublant, a French word that means "restless, troublesome, difficult." Tru thrashed about, working up into a swift current as the man boasted how he had "discovered" us. When Tru calmed down, we had a good laugh. How can someone discover something that's been around for ages? But the names stuck.

The surrounding town was called Renn Lake, and I felt honored to have an entire village named after me. Troublant was eventually shortened to Tru, which made my cousin happier, and that's how it is on maps today: the Tru River. We meet at my northern end, where Tru flows into me.

People have come and gone. Around us, Wisconsin spreads out in shades and hues and textures, reaching high and dipping low. Each day, the sun climbs and descends, and I wake and sleep to its constant rhythm.

The seasons blossom, then fade. Summers are busy and boisterous. Winters are snowy and quiet, a time for rest.

I am content.

For the most part.

There are times when I see something terrible, and I'm reminded how I can only stay still and watch. My heart ripples and sinks like a giant stone, then shatters into a thousand tiny pebbles, whirling aimlessly through my depths.

Like that day.

There was a moonless sky. A fragrant, overgrown garden. An open door. The bassinet.

It was just past dusk when I saw the woman. She was carrying a wrapped bundle in her arms. I wasn't quite sure what it was. Then a little hand poked out as she went around the outside of a store, toward the back. She was only gone a few minutes. When I saw her again, her arms were empty. At first, I thought she was bringing the bundle to someone. But I soon realized that wasn't the case. She slipped away, into the darkness.

The bundle was a baby girl.

I could not stay still and watch this time. *I must help,* I thought. *I must try.*

I gathered myself up and propelled a surge toward the

store. I landed with a loud slap, spraying the window. I startled the gray-haired figure who was inside sweeping the floor.

And the baby girl opened her tiny mouth and cried.

That was her beginning.

Chapter One

ANNALISE

"Jess! We have to get to the cabins. Come on!" As I open the screen door that leads to the porch, there's a muffled reply from my sister, somewhere upstairs. I bend over and reach underneath the wicker armchair to grab my flip-flops, then slip them on and go down the steps.

Jess is gesturing dramatically in front of her bedroom window. She pauses when she spots me, then opens it and yells down, "I'm in the middle of a scene, Annalise!"

"Hurry up and finish. Mom and Dad need our help."

She crosses her arms and stomps her foot. I can't quite see it, but I know. Always the right foot. With all the stomping Jess does, I don't know how her right leg isn't shorter than the left one by now.

"Why do we have to get there so early!" she shouts. "It's the first day of summer vacation!"

I'm about to remind her how much there is to do with all the guests checking in when I hear her thundering down the stairs. Jess says acting is her thing, not helping out with our family's rental cabins on the lake. But she's never tried out for anything—not at school or the community theater. Jess lets the screen door slam behind her. "Okay, fine. Let's go." She's wearing a gold-sequined tank top; a flouncy, satiny white skirt; and wedge sandals. She's also drawn major cat eyes with black liner and painted her fingernails neon green.

I tilt my head. "Why are you dressed like that?"

She twirls, then almost falls as she jumps over the steps. "Because I'm going to walk the red carpet." She skips around a puddle, then parades to the sidewalk while doing a little wave. I smile and catch up to her. So Jess.

She looks exactly like Mom did when she was little, with feathery hair, so light it's practically white, and skin that's almost transparent. I'm short, generously curvy, and have hazel eyes and pounds of dark ringlets. I don't look like anyone in my family.

I step over a fallen branch. "Did you hear the storm last night?"

"Uh-uh. I fell asleep with my headphones on."

"It was scary. I thought a window might break or something."

"Whoa. I'm glad I slept through it."

She stops and poses with a hand on her hip, one leg crossed in front of the other. "Oh, you're too kind. Yes,

I'm wearing a new designer. From Paris. Chloe Jeanette Le Grand."

"Is that really a designer?"

She laughs. "No."

We turn onto Sage Street. I've always wondered who named the streets in Renn Lake. There's Main, Church, and Park, but no other spice-related roads. Sage is a mystery. Like me.

We take Sage all the way to RL Middle. When we pass the building, it looks lonely, like it misses the kids. I'll be back there next year for seventh grade. Jess is going into fifth and has one more year at RL Elementary.

She stops her red-carpet walk and nudges me. "What's that boy doing?"

There's a tall, skinny boy I don't recognize standing in the center of the athletic field. He doesn't have a soccer ball or a baseball or anything. He's holding a book close up to his face.

"I don't know," I say.

"He looks kind of weird."

I glance at him again. "Interesting place to read."

"Yeah, really."

We keep walking, Jess wiggling her fingers and pointing to her neck. "Oh, my jewels? They're from a *very* expensive, *very* exclusive boutique. All the celebs go there."

I grin. "You're not just an actor, now you're a celeb?"

"Why not?"

When we reach Main Street, the large wooden sign proudly announces: WELCOME TO RENN LAKE, WISCONSIN'S BEST KEPT SECRET. Located halfway between Madison and the Illinois state line, Renn Lake is the town, and Renn Lake is the lake. They're symbiotic, like we learned about in science. They need each other.

Jess turns to me and makes a heart with her hands. "I forgot to tell you. Happy found day."

"Thanks." I catch a glimpse of Alden's at the end of Main across from the lake, innocent looking, like it's an ordinary store. I shiver a little, even though it's warm out.

Twelve years ago today.

Jess fixes her skirt, which has twisted around. "Another special dinner tonight. So yay, more cupcakes!" She sighs. "Honestly, the best part about you getting two celebrations is that I love cupcakes."

"Really?" I huff a little. Jess would say that.

She elbows me. "You know I'm only kidding."

We celebrate my birthday on June 2, the day the doctors determined I was born, and my found day on June 4. Mom and Dad started calling it that when I was five and they told me I was an abandoned baby. They would tickle my feet and sing a silly made-up song with rhymes for found day, like "homeward-bound day" and "astounding day" and "sounds like we love you day." They stopped tickling when I got older, but they still sing the song. Every year.

Even so, every year on this day, there's a hollow space in my chest that Mom and Dad's song can't quite fill.

I point to the sidewalk in front of the Main Street stores, wet and shiny from last night's rain. "It almost looks like an enchanted secret passageway, doesn't it? The way the sun is reflecting off the pavement."

Jess doesn't reply. She pauses in front of the movie theater and waves. To no one. "It's an honor just to be nominated," she gushes, giggling.

I smile. "You know you have to actually act in something before you're nominated?"

"I will!"

"Like you played the guitar and cooked with all those fancy utensils Mom and Dad bought you? What were they? A garlic press, right? And a lemon zester?"

"Don't make fun of me!" She zooms ahead.

I walk by Castaway, the secondhand shop, its white flag with the blue anchor waving lazily above the door, then the hardware and candy stores. Thick curls of ivy climb the front of the candy store, clinging tightly except for one long vine that lost its grip and is arching away from the building.

I stop just before the last store—Alden's Gift Emporium: Flora, Fauna, and Whatnot. I suppose I was Whatnot?

Faded reddish brick. The wood door with a stained-glass cutout. A water bowl on the ground for thirsty dogs. A striped awning. So normal. Nothing that would signify what happened here four thousand, three hundred, and eighty days ago. I've never gone inside. Mom or Dad might've taken me when I was little, but by myself? No.

I shade my eyes and scan the window. There are some plants, a gazing ball on a stand, and a kid-sized rocking chair, but . . . Mrs. Alden.

Jess pokes my arm. "What're you doing? I thought you said we had to hurry."

It hits me fresh. Mrs. Alden's gone. She died a month ago. Mr. Alden closed the store for a while and went to stay with one of his sons. But now, under the "Whatnot," it says: COME IN! WE'RE OPEN!

Every morning on found day, when I'd pass the store on the way to the cabins, Mrs. Alden would be in the window, like she was waiting for me. Did she know? Did she remember? She must have. She always gave me a soft smile, a nod. And I nodded back. A little thing. A big thing.

Mrs. Alden was the one who found me.

"Are you okay?" Jess asks. It feels like she's far away, and I'm inside a tunnel.

A tear escapes down my cheek, drips off my chin, and blends into the wet sidewalk. I've thought about it before, many times, but without Mrs. Alden in the window, it's like the view is clearer. My eyes are pulled into the store, to the back door, wide open to the garden. I picture a shadow carrying newborn me and then letting go. Putting me down. The shadow takes one step back. Then another. Then disappears.

It isn't just the *why,* which is bad enough, but there's the *how*—how did he, or she, lay me in the bassinet? Carefully? Angrily? In a rush? Did he, or she, look back? Worry that I might cry? Or did the person simply slip away without a concern, vanishing into the night?

Wisconsin's Best Kept Secret isn't Renn Lake.

Jess gently takes my hand. "C'mon, Annalise."

I shake off her hand and run across the street. I have to get to Renn.

At the edge, the water curls over my toes and I sort of melt down, my legs trembling, my whole body unsteady.

Shhh. You're okay.

My quick puffs of breath fade into the glassy blue surface.

It's just wood, brick, glass. It can't hurt you.

The water is warm, more like end-of-summer water. A few specks of green, the color of Jess's nail polish, catch in the sun.

Lap, lap, lap. A soothing rhythm circles around my legs, as if the lake is holding me. My breath starts to slow. The trembling fades.

You're safe. You're always safe here.

I don't actually hear Renn's words. I sense them. Feel them.

I have since I was three.

Chapter Two

RENN

"Annalise?" Her sister is standing near. "How come you took off?"

She wipes her eyes. "I don't know. I'm all right now. Go on. Tell Mom and Dad I'll be there in a minute."

"Okay." Her sister skips toward the row of cabins.

A baby linden leaf drifts toward Annalise and she leans forward, cups her hand, and carries it out. Some of them don't get to grow up. She places the leaf on her open palm and smooths it from edge to edge. A few geese fly overhead, flapping and squawking. The long reeds bend in the breeze and graze my surface. I hear laughter; two teenage boys are playing on my shore.

I wait.

The geese are long gone, black smudges far off in the sky, when Annalise says, "Why?" Her voice cracks, like a branch splitting from a tree. "Why, Renn? Why did someone abandon me?"

She's asked before. On her found days. After a ragged puppy was discovered wandering alone by my shore. Sometimes, strangely, on moonless nights. I always send soft, calming ripples but I never have an answer. After all this time, there is much I don't understand about people.

Annalise returns the leaf to my surface and I guide it gently on its way. We spend a few minutes in silence. A cloud moves across the sun, and she and I share the shade.

"Mrs. Alden's gone now," she whispers. "I can't talk to her, if I ever wanted to. She's the only one who might've seen. . . ."

My old heart aches. I dig through my treasures—there are many that have sunk to the bottom—keys, sunglasses, fossils, lots of canoe paddles. Things that were accidentally dropped into my wide-open arms, never to be seen again.

I can't offer her something special like my distant relatives Pacific and Atlantic. They could give her a whole peachy-white conch shell or a pointy shark's tooth. But I give her what I have. I bubble up an arrowhead and deposit it right by her knees.

Her face brightens as she picks it up. "Wow!" she says. "Look at this!"

I flow in delight.

She leaps up and runs toward the cabins. I watch

as she flings open the door to the office and shows the arrowhead to her parents. Her dad whistles, her mom oohs and aahs, then taps her finger on the tip.

"Let me see," Jess says, leaning in. "Cool, but I'm sure there's tons of arrowheads out there."

Not true. That was my only one.

Annalise's mom envelops her in a hug. I imagine their two hearts pressing together, each hearing the other's.

Tru and I have had many discussions about hearts. We have a simple one, directly in the deepest center, requiring only sunlight and oxygen to keep it going. People, I know, have a more complex heart. Ventricles, atriums, interconnected valves and muscles. And four separate chambers. Four, like the seasons, the winds, and the wings on a bumblebee.

I've thought long and hard about those four heart chambers. A brilliant design. If one should break, as it must have for Annalise when she was first told about being abandoned, there are still three others to rely on. But what about me and Tru, with our simple heart? What if it breaks?

"Tru?" I call softly.

No answer.

"Tru? Can you hear me?"

Tru is sluggish and steamy today. My cousin's a moody river, impulsive, changing course without warning. If

Tru doesn't feel like talking, there's a quiet, empty space between us.

Lately, I've been feeling warm too. The rain was heavy last night. An angry storm, sending debris and branches into my waters, ripping them into sharp fragments of driftwood.

When people are too warm, they jump in from the pier, wanting me to cool their reddened skin. But I've wondered, what will cool me if I stay this warm?

The days are getting longer now. The pines are shedding their brittle needles and the lindens are caring for their young saplings. Soon, people will fill up my shore from end to end. I rustle my ancient, watery bones. Time to get ready for summer.

Chapter Three

ANNALISE

Mom's holding me so tight, my nose is smooshed against her T-shirt. "Happy found day, sweetheart," she says.

"Thanks."

She lets go but puts her hands on the sides of my shoulders and sniffles a little. "Twelve. I still can't believe it. How did that happen?"

"It happened because you can't stop it from happening," Jess answers, spinning, making her skirt flare out.

Dad hugs me too; then they glance at each other and launch into their found day rhyming song, with Jess humming along, pretending she's holding a microphone. I let them go, until they finish on a long, drawn-out note and round of applause. They beam at me and I try to smile back.

I slide the arrowhead into my shorts pocket. It feels smooth and flat against the fabric. When I take out my hand, I realize it's shaking. Walking by Alden's, I always felt kind of uncomfortable, a little tragic and wounded, but I never saw that shadow inside.

Mom studies my face. "What's wrong? Are you getting too old for this now that you're almost a teenager?"

I clasp my hands to steady them. "No, no."

"Even if you are," Dad says, "we're going to keep singing and embarrassing you."

Jess laughs. "Even when she's, like, ninety?"

"Even then," Dad replies.

How could I ever tell them to stop? Mom and Dad tried for years to have a baby. Then I appeared. A miracle, they said. Jess was a surprise. Mom got pregnant one year later.

"I always feel bad that your birthday and found day are at the beginning of the season, when we're so busy," Mom says. "But we'll celebrate tonight at dinner. The usual found day menu: mac 'n' cheese and cupcakes with sprinkles. Your favorites."

"Cupcakes!" Jess shouts.

Dad looks at her. "Nice outfit."

She rolls her eyes.

Dad goes to the ladder in the corner, climbs up, and unscrews a light bulb. His head practically touches the ceiling. He's tall—six three—and his hair is wispy, like loose pieces of thread. Mom's tall too, five ten, and her hair is darker than Jess's and cut short. They're both thin and freckly. The only jewelry they wear is their plain, slim gold wedding bands.

When I was starting kindergarten, they told me that I was adopted before some kid in class blurted it out. I asked Mom what she thought I was. My heritage, I meant. I could be a blend of anything, really.

She explained that I could do a DNA test to find out when I was older, but for now, I shouldn't spend time worrying about it. "One of the most beautiful things in the world is its mysteries," she said. "The unknown."

I went to Renn that day. It was almost September, and the cabins were quiet. Just a few last guests. I unbuckled my white sandals and planted my toes on the sandy shore. I peered into the water, trying to see below the surface. The water was a little cloudy, but then I spotted a school of tiny fish darting back and forth. Renn bubbled around them, like they were playing. I smiled and dipped my hand in, but the fish swam off. I remember looking toward the other shore, thinking there must be lots of fish swimming in the lake, even though I couldn't see them.

Mom ducks behind the front desk and when she pops up, she's holding something behind her back. Dad gets down from the ladder. They both have sneaky smiles, like they can barely hold in a secret.

"What?" I look from one to the other.

Mom hands me a small wrapped box. They always give me a present on found day. I tear the paper and carefully lift the cover. Inside is a delicate necklace, with a tiny house pendant. Silver, with a triangular roof, two windows, and a door etched in the metal. It swings gently back and forth from my fingers like a pendulum, catching little house-shaped squares of light.

"I saw it when I was in Madison last month," Mom says. "I fell in love with it, just like I fell in love with you the first time I saw you and brought you home." She gulps, puts a hand across her throat. "But it's returnable, if you don't like it—"

"No, I love it." I undo the clasp and put it on. "How does it look?"

She lets out a breath. "Perfect. Just beautiful. I think it was meant for you."

Dad nods. "Agree."

"Pretty," Jess says, then sighs. "So what am I doing? Welcome bags?"

"Yes." Mom points to the table by the front door. "I already started. There's just a few more coupons to add."

Jess walks over to the table, picks up a stack of coupons, then fans them out like cards. "Anyone have a five?"

Dad laughs. "Go fish."

Jess starts dropping coupons into the small paper bags lined up on the table.

The office phone rings and Mom takes the call, pulling up the reservation calendar on her laptop. Dad looks over her shoulder as she types. "Another booking," he says. "We're full until the second week in August."

"Awesome," I say. "It's going to be a great summer!"

Mom finishes typing the information, then hangs up. "We certainly need one. The last few were so slow. I was beginning to think no one wanted to stay at sleepy old cabins anymore. Not when there's water parks and all the attractions in the Dells."

"We could build a water park here," Jess says, rearranging the bags by color.

"We could," Dad answers. "If we had a few million dollars to spare." He scans the laptop screen. "It cost us an arm and a leg, but maybe the ads we put in those vacation guides really worked."

I glance at Dad. "How much did they cost?"

"A lot. But if we keep getting bookings, it was worth it. I think we can get those three cabin roofs repaired now. We didn't have enough money last year."

"And let's replace the windows," Mom adds. "The ones that are leaking. It's never-ending, keeping this place up." She smiles. "But I wouldn't trade it for anything."

When Mom's grandpa was young and first came to Wisconsin, he bought some land around the lake and built the cabins. He passed them down to Mom's dad, who passed them down to Mom. There's a picture of the three of them above the fireplace at home. Mom was around eight. They're standing proudly in front of the office, in the shade of a pine tree. Bands of sunlight are poking through the branches, and their arms are around each other's waists.

The cabins have been here so long, it's as if they've sunken in and become part of the earth, like the grass and the soil and the lake. When I'm inside them, enveloped in their woody smell, their roots beneath my feet, Alden's, across the street from the lake, seems miles away. Harder to believe.

Mom pushes a strand of hair off her forehead. "Annalise, I know it's your found day, and maybe you wanted to hang out with Maya later, but Vera's out sick. I haven't had a minute to check if she got to all the bed linens and towels—"

"Maya's visiting her aunt and uncle in Milwaukee until tomorrow." I grab the ring of keys from the front desk drawer. "I'm on it."

Mom hands me the clipboard with each cabin listed, and little boxes to check off for clean sheets, towels, fresh bars of soap, vacuuming, and emptying trash. "Thank you. I'll send Jess over to help when she's done with the bags."

"I can do reservations," Jess pipes up.

"No," Mom and Dad blurt at the same time.

"I won't delete any this time, I promise."

Dad pats her shoulder. "Maybe next year."

Jess reads one of the coupons. "Ten percent off a smoothie. Does anyone even use these? I mean, can't the stores get apps or something? Because that would be the way to go, if you want my opinion."

"Good idea, Jess, but I don't think they can afford that," Mom says, turning back to her laptop.

"Maybe we can get an app. For, like, reservations. People could just click and come."

"Maybe . . . ," Mom says.

"I mean, you know, when the windows are fixed and stuff." Jess drops the coupon into a bag. I tuck the clipboard under my arm and go out, then head straight to cabin 1, which is closest to the office. Vera's worked here as long as I can remember, and while I don't want her to be sick, I'm glad to be busy.

Cabin 1 has a king-sized bed, made perfectly, the blanket tucked in tight. I check the living room, kitchen, and bathroom; all neat and ready for the next guests. Cabins 2 and 3 are in good shape too, but cabin 4 is missing everything—no sheets, pillowcases, or towels. And I catch a whiff of dirty socks. I find two on the floor next to the bed, plus a sweatshirt on a chair, and a pacifier on the bathroom sink.

People always leave stuff behind. We throw everything into a lost-and-found bin in the office. No one ever comes back for their things, so I don't know why Mom and Dad hold on to them.

I take the socks, sweatshirt, and pacifier to the bin, then grab what I need from the supply closet. Back in cabin 4, I drop everything on an armchair, then open a window to get the smell out. The carpet is damp near the window. This must be one that's leaking. I arrange the towels in the bathroom—layering them big to small, all folded in thirds. I am a towel master.

I fling the mattress cover across the bed, then lift each corner, pulling the cover underneath, snug and tight. Jess seems so certain about acting (for now), but it's hard to imagine myself being *something*. A doctor? A teacher? A sheepherder? I will say this, though. If my career involves anything to do with bedding and towels, I'm golden.

I go from cabin to cabin—there are twelve in total—and only 8 and 11 are also in need of bed-making/towel-hanging. I don't come across any more left-behind things except three pennies and a quarter, which I immediately claim. Since I started helping with the cabins a few years ago, any coins I find go into a glass jar in my room. When

I last counted my haul, I had sixteen dollars and seventy-two cents. I'm saving it for something. I don't know what yet.

As I'm finishing up the last cabin, Jess waltzes in. "Hey."

"Where've you been?"

"Sorrryyy. I was tying ribbons on the bags."

"This whole time?"

"Yeah. I was curling them. Making the presentation more appealing. That's what it's about, you know." She snorts. "Mom made me use little kid scissors."

I scan the clipboard. "Well, I'm done."

On the way back to the office, Jess elbows me. "There's that weird boy again. The one who was by your school."

She's right. He's kneeling next to a tree. He has longish brown wavy hair in a ponytail and is even skinnier up close. He's hunched over the dirt and peering through a magnifying glass. I hear him mutter, "Not good. Definitely not good."

I wonder what he means. But he's completely immersed in whatever he's looking at, so I continue to the office. Dad's on the phone and Mom is putting some Sharpies into a Renn Lake Rentals coffee cup.

"Done," I announce. "Every cabin is ready. Except four, eight, and eleven need vacuuming. I forgot to take the vacuum with me."

Mom waves a hand. "I'll do that. Terrific. Thank you." She gives me the cup and Jess a stack of sticky notes. "You two want to inaugurate the Thought Wall this year?"

"Sure." I pick a blue Sharpie and Jess grabs an orange one.

There's a wall in the office where people can put up notes with messages. They write the craziest, most hilarious, strangest, sweetest things. Mom even had a plaque made that says: "Hi, I am a wall. Fill me with your thoughts."

I peel off a paper square, then glance back at Mom and Dad. Sometimes their faces crease over with this nervous look, and they have it now. Like they worry that one random day, maybe one found day, I'm going to suddenly explode and scream: *Someone left me in a store when I was an infant! I am really not okay!* then fall down a black hole.

Jess scribbles something, then sticks her note to the wall, the first one for this year. It says: *JessiKa was here.*

Mom, Dad, and I look at it.

"What?" she asks. "I'm thinking of changing the spelling of my name. If I'm going to be a famous actor, I need to be unique."

Mom sighs. "We'll see." Dad pats the top of Jess's head. "A capital *K,* huh?"

"Yes. Unique."

I touch the house necklace, then write: *One of the most beautiful things in the world is the unknown.* I put it on the wall too.

"Good one," Dad says.

"Indeed," Mom adds.

Their faces are back to normal.

I stare at what I wrote. Most of the time I am okay. But what would have happened if Mrs. Alden hadn't been there? What if no one had found me?

Chapter Four

RENN

They are here.

A dizzying array of blankets and towels are spread along my shore. Umbrellas are stuck into the sandy earth, chairs underneath them, and everywhere there are bags overflowing with food. People seem to be hungry all the time.

They jump from the end of the pier, sending splashes into the air, and they float on rafts, their noses painted white to block the sun. Their words bounce and echo, skimming my surface and landing on my edges. *Lemonade. Canoe. Goggles.*

Tru and I, and other bodies of water, communicate with sound too, but it moves through waves and currents, not the air. And sometimes, things are simply understood, from one to the other.

Many of their words are confusing. *Lollipop. Balloon.*

Hairdresser. And *bassinet.* I asked my cousin about that one. Why would a container to hold a baby be described as a *fish* in a *net*? Tru smiled and explained the word has nothing to do with a fish or a net. It's from the French. *Bassinet,* Tru said, means "little basin."

That made more sense. And I realized it's another connection between Annalise and me.

I am a big basin; she was left in a small one.

There is only a small number of people who have talked to me and could hear me. Most of them were long ago, when I was Nepew. One, a girl who studied plants and learned to use them for healing. Another, a hunter, who dropped the arrowhead into me.

I remember well the first time Annalise heard me. She was three years old. With a yellow shovel clutched in her chubby fist, she was digging in the sand. When I trickled over her feet, she looked up and laughed. She watched me flow away, leaving bubbles behind, and she laughed again. "Renn," she said.

I answered, unsure. *Hello.*

She stood, came closer, waved. "Hi, Renn."

Her mother, nearby, asked who she was talking to. Annalise pointed at me. "The lake." Her mother smiled and continued to feed Jess with a tiny spoon.

Annalise kneeled and pulled out a soggy plastic bag

that had wound its way into my shallow waters. "Garbage," she said, and carried it to a trash can.

When she came back, I said: *Thank you.*

She patted my surface with the palm of her hand. "You're welcome."

My heart glowed—she hears me! But as I watched her leave that day with her mother and sister, I worried that she would forget, or stop believing, or outgrow me, like I was an imaginary friend. Instead, she began coming to me on her found days, and other times, when she needed comfort, like the afternoon she overheard two women standing in front of Alden's. "I remember reading in the paper years ago that a baby was abandoned here," one said. The other replied, "Such a terrible thing. I hope that baby's all right."

Annalise ran to me. Tears slid down her cheeks and dropped into my waters. I gathered them up and made them disappear. I told her she was all right, again and again, until she was.

There's a commotion on my shore. Several young people are pointing to the ground. I realize what they're gawking at. I'd seen it floating earlier. A fish. Yellow and black scales, lying limply on one side, a glassy round eye staring up at nothing.

Fish die, of course. It's part of the cycle. But usually, when they're done living. I remember this one being born in the spring, along with her brothers and sisters. I know her mother. I knew her grandmother, and her grandmother. And many before them.

There's a tiny speck of algae on the tail. I'd noticed some algae this morning, in a quiet cove near the reeds. Sticky and thick like tree sap, the color of a lime caterpillar. It felt different than regular algae. Fizzy. Dense. When I tried to nudge it, it didn't move. Underneath it, my waters were perfectly still.

A small girl with copper-colored hair studies the fish. "It looks sad," she says. "Why isn't it swimming?"

My insides rumble and swirl, and I feel uneasy. I give fish a home, keep them safe. I always have. But I let this one down.

Chapter Five

ANNALISE

Dad and I are planting geraniums in the window boxes outside the office. Jess was helping but after she dug a few holes and put in the flowers, she insisted she had to go home and "rehearse."

"For your Broadway debut?" Dad winked.

"No, Hollywood!" she called as she ran off.

I stuffed in a flower and packed the dirt around it. "She always gets out of things."

He gently loosened a geranium from the plastic tray. "She's only ten. You weren't so dedicated at that age either. And besides, sometimes it's just easier not to argue with her."

I laughed. "True."

We hear some shouts coming from the lake and I see a bunch of kids huddled at the shore. Dad looks over. "Let's go see what's happening," he says.

We walk toward the group, and when I get close, I hear

a boy say "Gross!" and another boy yell "Cool!" They're both poking at something with sticks. The tall, skinny boy with the ponytail is on the edge of the crowd. Is he staying in one of the cabins? I don't remember seeing him check in.

"What's going on?" Dad asks, motioning for the kids to step back. Then I see a dead fish lying on its side with its mouth stuck open.

A small red-haired girl tugs the bottom edge of Dad's shorts. "Mr. Oliver? Did the fish die?"

"I'm afraid so," Dad answers.

"How come?" she asks.

"I don't know, honey. We can't always know the answer to things."

She frowns. Her lower lip trembles. "But it needs to swim in the water. That's what fish do. Can't you give it some medicine?"

He shakes his head. Then an older woman calls to the girl. "C'mon, Sophie." Her grandma, I think. They checked in to cabin 4 today.

"I'll be right back," Dad tells me, and hurries toward the office. I scan the water. I don't see any other dead fish. I wish I could say something to Renn, but I can't right now. Not with all the people around.

Dad returns with a pail and quickly scoops up the fish. "Okay," he says to the kids. "All taken care of." They slowly scatter, the two boys dragging their sticks through the sand. The tall boy with the ponytail brushes past me. "Could be a sign," he mutters. A sign of what?

I don't want to look at the fish, so I walk on the other side of Dad, away from the pail. When we reach the office, he heads around back to the dumpster and I go inside.

"What happened?" Mom asks.

"Dead fish. Washed up on the shore."

She comes out from behind the front desk, and puts her arm around my shoulders. "Why don't you go home? You've been working hard all day. Dad and I will be there soon for our special dinner." She kisses my cheek.

"Okay." I start to go out, then glimpse Alden's across the street. I rush back in. My eyes dart around the room and my hands are shaking.

"Forget something?" Mom asks.

"No . . ." I don't know what to do. I have to pass the store on my way home, there's no other route. What if I see that shadow again?

Mom tilts her head. "Annalise?"

I spot the rack of Renn Lake Rentals caps by the desk. Mom had a whole bunch made last year, thinking they'd be good advertising, but not many people bought them. When I was five, right after they'd explained how Mrs. Alden found me, I insisted on wearing a winter hat with a pom-pom and long tassels every single day, even in warm weather. I'd come across it at Castaway when I was there with Mom. It'd been misplaced, hidden and alone under a rack of dresses, and I was positive it was meant for me. I pretended it was an armor helmet that protected me against bad things.

I point. "Can I have a cap?"

"Sure, of course." She takes a purple one and gives it to me.

I squash it down over my curls, then go out again and hurry toward Main. I zoom by the building, cap pulled low, head down. I let out a long breath when I'm past. Nothing. But I keep the cap on the whole way just in case.

When I get to my block, my phone buzzes. It's a text from Maya. We've been best friends since third grade when she moved into the house in back of mine.

"Going crazy here! I'm the only kid. They've done three things so far. Sit, talk, and eat."

"Ugh! You'll be home soon."

"Don't do anything fun without me."

"I won't."

"OMG. Now my mom wants me to play the piano for my aunt. The piece from my recital that I can't even remember! HELP."

I send some laughing emojis but she doesn't respond.

I reach our house, with its peeling blue paint, loose shutters, and crooked mailbox, and feel grateful that I'm here.

Jess is in the porch swing, hands clasped in her lap. She's wiped off the eyeliner and changed into shorts and a T-shirt. I drop into the armchair next to her.

She touches a foot to the floor and rocks the swing, her baby-chick hair lifting and falling with the motion. "I've made a huge decision."

"Oh yeah? What is it?"

"I'm for sure changing the spelling of my name. *J-E-S-S-I,* capital *K-A.* I just finished redoing all my social media accounts."

"What's wrong with Jess?"

"Regular names don't cut it in the acting world. This will make me stand out. I mean, who's going to remember Jess Oliver? And no last name either, like all the famous one-name celebrities. JessiKa." She says it in a whispery, breathy voice.

I can't help it, I laugh.

She bolts up, plunks her hands on her hips. "It's not funny, Annalise! You have no idea. You have to start young. You have to know what you're doing if you're truly serious. And I am."

"Jess—"

"iKa!"

"Right. Sorry. Um . . . are you sure about this? I mean, you've never taken a class or been in a school play—"

"School plays aren't for serious actors. They do, like"—she snorts—"*The Wizard of Oz.*"

"What's wrong with *The Wizard of Oz*? Everyone loves it."

She brushes a hand at me. "It's so *boring*. So *done*. And of course I'm sure!"

She said that about playing guitar in a band and hosting her own cooking show. There was something else too, but I can't remember.

Jess(iKa) climbs onto the swing, stands on the seat, then grabs the chains as the swing wobbles. "And you know what else? When Mom and Dad get old, I'm *not* taking over the cabins. They're all yours." She points to the cap. "I see how much you love them."

I get goosebumps.

"I'll probably be in LA, anyway," Jess says. "Palm trees and swimming pools. And the ocean, of course. No lakes."

"I think there are lakes in California."

Jess shrugs, jumps down from the swing, then leans over the porch railing and peers out, like she wishes she could be carried off by the wind to LA right now.

"How come you want to leave so badly?" I ask softly.

"How come you don't?" She sweeps her arm in a half circle. "I want to go everywhere!"

I trace the necklace with the tip of one finger. Houses like ours are across the street. Rows of trees and squares of lawn and parallel gray sidewalks. Jess taped pictures of Rome and Tokyo and Paris all over her room, but in my room there's a big frame with photos of the lake, the cabins, me and Maya, and one from last year's Fourth of July Fest. And my jar of found coins on my dresser, more than half-filled now.

Mom and Dad pull into the driveway and Jess races down the steps. "I'm going with JessiKa for sure, okay? With a capital *K*. So can you call me that from now on?"

Mom ruffles her hair. "We'll talk about that, honey. Right now, it's Annalise's found day dinner."

Jess stomps her foot. Dad grins. "Do we put an emphasis on the *K* when we say it, so people know? Jess-i-*KUH*?" He stomps his foot too.

"Yeah, that'll work," she says, and he laughs.

We go into the kitchen. Mom pulls a pan of mac 'n' cheese from the fridge and puts it in the oven. Dad starts slicing tomatoes for a salad. Jess opens a drawer and takes out a stack of index cards and a pen. She plops down on a chair and starts scribbling *Love, JessiKa* on each one, surrounding the letters with stars and flowers.

"What are those for?" I ask.

"I'm practicing my autograph." She offers me a card. "Hold on to this, it'll be valuable one day."

I take the card and slide it into my shorts pocket, along with the quarter and pennies. The arrowhead is still in the other pocket.

Thirty minutes later, we're all at the table with bubbling mac 'n' cheese, cornbread, and salad. The cupcakes are waiting on the counter.

We start to eat, and Jess's phone buzzes. "I know, no phones at dinner, but this might be important." She scrolls, then gasps and nearly chokes. "This is IT!"

"This is what?" Mom says.

I lean over to glance at her screen, but she covers it with her hand. "So, okay, I have this app that sends alerts for auditions, and there's one in Madison! For a movie! They need local extras." She claps a hand over her heart. "Can I go? Please say I can go."

Dad takes a big spoonful of mac 'n' cheese, piles it onto his plate. "In Madison? When is it?"

"Hold on," Mom says. "Just a second. Jess—"

"iKa."

"Jess-*iKa.* It's great that you're interested in acting. But you know we're at the beginning of our busy season. One of us might possibly be able to take you to the audition, but don't hundreds of kids go to these things? If you even got a part, and I'm guessing that's a long shot, how would we get you there? We can't take time off right now."

Jess waves her fork. "Easy-peasy. One, don't worry, I could take a bus to the audition. Two, if I got a part, we could work everything out. They probably have a trailer for the extras to stay in."

Mom rubs her forehead. "You can't take a bus. Or stay in a trailer. You're ten years old."

She holds up her phone. "That's exactly the age they need."

"Maybe you could start a little smaller and closer to home," Dad suggests. "Try out for the school play in the fall. Then we'll see about movies."

I elbow her. "I heard they're doing *The Wizard of Oz* next year."

Jess pushes her plate aside. "I don't want to be in a school play. I want to go big. This could be my way to break in."

Mom says in a firm voice, "We took you to that kids' cooking show tryout, and you quit after you didn't make it. And the guitar—"

My sister crosses her arms. "This isn't like those other things! You guys just don't get me. Sometimes I wonder why I'm in this family."

Mom raises an eyebrow and gives her a long look. "That's not a very nice thing to say."

"It's true we can't choose our family," Dad says, glancing at me. "Except in special circumstances."

Something flickers across Jess's face and she huffs.

"Anyway, Jess, enough of this right now," Mom says. "It's Annalise's day."

She slides down in her chair so she's eye level with the table. "iKa," she mutters.

Mom picks up her glass. "Let's all wish Annalise a happy found day." They do, again, and Jess mumbles something that sounds like "happy fun day."

Last year on my found day, Jess insisted that she'd sprained her arm in gym. (She hadn't.) The year before that, she wanted a certain kind of strawberry lip gloss and wouldn't stop begging Mom and Dad to get her one. I figure they see it, but like Dad said, sometimes it's just easier not to argue with her. She's like a mini tornado sometimes.

The rest of the dinner is awkward, with Jess sulking and Mom smiling too much. "We can have the cupcakes on the porch," Mom says, handing me the box after we've finished. "You two go out; we'll be there in a minute." She starts clearing the dishes.

I put the box on the table and sit in the swing. Jess drops onto the chair. There's a blurry circle of moon, and the air is hot and still.

Jess touches the edge of the table with her toes. "If it was you wanting to go to the audition, they'd have said yes in a second." Her voice is soft, croaky.

I run my hand over the fabric outline of the arrowhead. "I'm not so sure," I say, even though she's probably right.

"I mean, I *get it.*"

Do you, though? I wonder.

"They're so different with you," Jess says. "It's everything . . . even our names. You have the beloved grandmothers, Anna and Elise, and I'm named after the crazy aunt who talked to the furniture." Her words hang between us. She looks at me, her eyes watery. "My stomach hurts. I don't think I want a cupcake."

She gets up and goes to the door, then stops. "What were you doing this morning, when you were staring at the store? It was like you were in a trance. Were you thinking about . . . you know?"

I shake my head and stare at the wood planks on the floor. I don't want to tell her, or anyone, what I saw, what I imagined.

She stands there for a few seconds, then goes inside. I take the arrowhead, the coins, and the card with Jess's autograph out of my pockets and put them on top of the cupcake box.

The best thing about found day? When it's over.

The night I was discovered, they thought it was a mistake. Because who would actually leave a baby in a store? A person can leave a newborn at a fire station or a hospital if they aren't wanted or can't be cared for. But a gift shop?

The police searched for fingerprints and conducted an investigation. There was a 1-800 tip line, news stories, and flyers taped in windows and on bulletin boards. I was a little famous.

I once read a short story for school about this boy who'd been abandoned as an infant. He was searching for his birth mother, and when he finally found her, there was a big, emotional scene at the end. I couldn't understand it. Why go looking for someone who threw you away? Dropped you off like they were returning you, like you didn't fit or they changed their mind. Like you were a discard. Like you meant nothing.

I'm not going to search. Not now. Not ever.

Chapter Six

RENN

The night I first saw baby Annalise was peaceful and quiet. The people had gone home.

The woman walked from the store, her arms empty, her shoulders sagging. I noticed the bassinet near the back door, open to the small garden, scented with lilies and roses. The woman continued toward me, stepping softly onto my shore. Then she turned and moved toward the lindens.

The canoe wasn't on a rack with the others, but was concealed in a ribbon of long grass under one of the trees. That afternoon had been exceptionally busy at the canoe tent. Groups of twos and threes had paddled out one after the other. I hardly had a moment's calm.

She approached the hidden canoe and stood by its side for a long moment. Had she tucked it away there? I couldn't remember seeing her before.

Pushing it across the grass to my shore, she waded in, her long skirt billowing around her like a sail. I couldn't see the woman's face; there was no moon that night. She steadied the canoe, climbed in, reached for the paddle inside, and began to stroke.

The cattails on my eastern side bent in concern. The lindens nervously rattled their leaves and crackled their roots. I sent a gentle wave toward the woman. Then several more. *Go back,* I hoped they said. *Go back to shore. It's much too dark and much too late to be out here with me.*

A mounting panic rose from my depths, from way down in my mucky bottom, as she continued to carve the oar. In. Out. Back. Forth. Again, again, again. I could sense that her arms were beginning to tire but she kept going. Farther and farther away. In the direction of Tru.

I sent the surge toward the store, then attempted to bring the woman back to my shore without toppling the canoe. I tried.

Inside the store, Viv Alden lifted the crying baby and began to soothe her.

I watched the woman as long as I could. Her silhouette gliding across my surface under the black sky, the paddle barely making a sound as it dipped below. She became smaller and smaller.

In the end, Tru took her. I called out to my cousin, but either Tru didn't hear or chose not to. And then the woman was gone.

No matter how many times I've asked, Tru has never answered my questions about that night.

Chapter Seven

ANNALISE

The next morning, I drop the new coins into my jar, put the arrowhead and iKa's autograph card on my dresser, then knock on my sister's bedroom door. "You ready?"

"I'll come later."

"I can wait for you."

"No. I still have a stomachache."

"Listen . . . maybe I can talk to Mom and Dad about the audition."

"I don't want you to. Just go."

I shake my head. "Fine." I grab the cap and put it on. It worked yesterday. I'm not taking any chances.

When I'm on Main, Toni waves to me from the door of Castaway and I wave back. There's a banner below the movie theater marquee that says FREE POPCORN WITH TICKET PURCHASE! The long strand of ivy is dangling from the brick of the candy shop. Seems like it's barely hanging on.

I'm hurrying past Alden's, doing my best not to look, but a burst of pink in the window catches my eye. It's a flock of inflatable flamingo floaties with inner tubes. On their long necks, it says ALDEN'S GIFTS. They're standing on fake grass but seem a little unsteady. One of them starts to lean, then falls over, knocking down the whole row in slow motion until they're a messy pile of pink.

Mr. Alden must've tried to do the display. Everyone in town always admired Mrs. Alden's windows. Kites that looked as if they were really flying. A stuffed animal family having a Fourth of July picnic. A row of knitted mittens strung up during the holidays, each one with a face. If Mrs. Alden were here, she would've figured out a way to get those flamingos to stay in place.

My heart speeds up and I start to get that feeling like I'm in a tunnel again, and being pulled inside. I tug the cap lower and race across the street. When I reach the lake, I go close to the edge and whisper "Good morning" to Renn. The shore is already getting filled up with people.

Good morning to you.

I stand there, my reflection flickering in the water, until my heart slows and I feel like I'm on firmer ground. I dip in my hand, then take it out, watching the water drip from the ends of my fingers and back into Renn. I do it a few more times, until Alden's, behind me, loosens its grip and the shadowy space of where I came from floats away.

"Thanks," I whisper.

When I come into the office, Mom says, "Where's Jess?" and I tell her. Mom calls her, asking if her forehead feels warm or if she threw up. I can hear Jess saying no to both. "Rest and drink a lot," Mom instructs, and says she'll come home as soon as she can to check on her.

Vera's still not here, so I'm on bed-and-towel duty again, plus the official suitcase carrier, refunder of quarters eaten by the soda machine, and admirer of Thought Wall sticky notes. More have been added:

Whoever invented Mountain Dew was a genius.

Friendship is not a ship.

Just keep swimming. Literally.

I confess to nothing.

Mom and Dad are constantly busy, taking care of little things (fixing the TV in cabin 5), big things (a clogged, overflowing toilet in cabin 9), and everything in between (a bee in the office, someone who dropped their key in the lake). We have a lot of extra bug spray and even more spare keys.

I finally get a chance to check my phone in the afternoon, and there's a long string of texts from Maya, who's back in town and starting her summer babysitting job.

"PLEASE come out to the lake when you can. I'm here and it's not good. Henry has said poop-head 30 times, Tyler has said fart-face 50 times. They told me I'm the meanest babysitter they've ever had and they hate me. Is this seriously worth 10 bucks an hour?"

I poke my head out of the office door and scan the shore. I spot her and the two boys, then ask Mom if I can take a break.

"Of course," she says, rifling through some papers.

When I reach Maya, she's glaring at the two boys with her hands on her hips. Her bun is a mess, loose strands everywhere, and she's got a smear of something on her cheek. Dried banana, maybe?

She collapses into a hug, pulls back, and clutches my shoulders. "Annalise! What was I thinking? That stupid babysitting class didn't prepare me for anything!"

I laugh as she lets go. "Classes never teach you what you really need to know, right?"

One of the boys says, "Hey! We're not babies!" He thumps the other boy's chest with his fist and Maya quickly grabs his arm. "Henry! Don't do that! Didn't I tell you, no hitting. Be nice to each other. Haven't you guys heard of kindness and all that stuff?"

"You're not the boss of me, Maya Levine!" Henry says. "You can't tell me what to do!" Tyler sticks out his tongue. "Yeah! Me either."

I point to Maya's face. "You've got some . . ."

She wipes her cheek. "Now I see why Mrs. Olsen hired me on the spot. They're seven-year-old twin monsters. She couldn't wait to get rid of them." She takes two plastic bottles of juice from a cooler and holds them above the boys' heads. "If you sit on the blanket and drink these nicely and quietly, I will give you back your lightsabers later, okay?"

The boys plop onto the blanket and Maya hands them the juice. "Nicely!" she repeats. They rip off the caps and slurp noisily.

"If every day's going to be like this, I don't know how I'll survive, Annalise. My brother's so lucky he got to go to sleepaway camp."

"It can't be that bad."

"Um, it can."

I smile. "As bad as a blimperfly?"

She smiles too. "Now, *that* was bad."

In third grade, right after we met, we teamed up for an art assignment. We had to use papier mâché to create something that could fly, but it had to be half animal, half machine. We designed a cross between a blimp and butterfly. We called it a blimperfly. Our papier mâché mixture was full of clumps and the wings wouldn't attach. Calling it a disaster would be kind. Since then, we tell each other that nothing's ever as bad as a blimperfly.

“That reminds me,” she says, digging in her backpack and pulling out a giant multicolored gummy butterfly. “Sorry I missed your birthday.”

“Ha! This is great.” I rip open the package and take a bite. “Thanks.” I offer it to her.

She takes a bite too, then tucks a few strands of hair into her bun. “Well, at least we can hang out here a lot. That should take up some time.”

I stuff the gummy into my shorts pocket and notice a dad and little girl near us. He’s helping her step into a flamingo floatie, like the ones in the Alden’s window. She toddles down to the water, one flamingo leg dragging behind her.

“Why do flamingos stand on one leg anyway?” I say aloud, not sure if I meant to.

Henry burps. “That’s how they rest their muscles and keep warm, don’t you know anything?”

Maya and I stare at him. “Is that true?” she asks, narrowing her eyes.

“Yeah. I read it. In a book about flamingos. I did a report for school.”

Tyler’s nodding. “Henry’s smart. Smarter than anyone in the whole world.” Tyler’s got a purple juice mustache that makes him look like a cartoon villain.

The little girl reaches the lake, shakes her head, shouts

"No!" and steps out of the floatie. Her dad kneels down, pats her shoulder, gestures to the water. She shakes her head again and tosses the flamingo aside. A curly-haired boy picks it up and the girl points at him, then starts wailing. Her dad retrieves the flamingo and when he brings it back, she hugs it like it's a long-lost friend, pulls it up around her middle, and wades happily into the lake.

Henry stands, burps again, and gives Maya his empty bottle. "We want our lightsabers back."

Maya holds up the bottle. "After you put this in the recycling can."

Henry actually does it, then comes back and sticks out his hand.

"I'm going to regret this." Maya takes two lightsabers from her backpack. "Okay, now listen—"

The boys grab them and run toward the lake, slashing the air and jabbing each other.

"I know you have to get back to the cabins, but please stay with me a little longer," Maya pleads. "I'm begging you. I might go insane."

"Sure."

We sprint after them, Maya yelling, "Would you guys chill?"

We're far down the shore when I stop to catch my breath. That always makes me think of literally trying to grab a handful of my breath as it blows out and hold on to it. Shouldn't it be more like, stop to *slow* your breath?

Something bright green is on top of the water by the reeds. Like a clump of leaves. But when I get closer, I see that it's a slick, syrupy coating, so thick I can't make out the water underneath. Almost like wet paint.

Henry and Tyler are suddenly next to me. "Slime!" Henry cries. "Awesome!"

Tyler pinches his nose. "It smells yucky, like our basement!"

"What is this?" I say. "I've never seen something like this in the lake before."

Henry's about to dip his lightsaber into the green stuff but Maya reaches over to stop him. "I don't think that's a good idea."

Henry crosses his arms. "How come you won't let us do *anything*?"

"Deal with it," Maya snaps. "Safety first, that's how I roll."

I giggle, covering my mouth. "That's how you *roll*?"

"You wouldn't believe the things I've been coming up with. 'This is for your own good.' 'I'm not going to say it again.' I even called them meshuggeners."

"What's that?"

"Crazy, in Yiddish. My aunt spoke Yiddish the whole time I was there. She said it won't be a dead language if people use it. I guess it worked because now *I'm* saying the words!"

I laugh. "It's a great word, though."

"And you know what else? My parents handed out dental floss to the entire family! Apparently, it wasn't enough to give it out at Halloween and embarrass me in front of everyone I know." She sighs. "It's not easy being the daughter of not one but two dentists."

"Hey, at least you have great teeth."

She groans.

A twig snaps behind me and I turn around. The boy with the ponytail is standing there. Even though he's really tall, his face looks around my age.

He walks toward the water. "Just as I suspected." He takes a magnifying glass from his shorts pocket, crouches, and examines the green covering.

"What are you doing?" I ask.

"This mat of blue-green algae," he says. "Could be the start of a dead zone."

"A *dead zone*?" Maya repeats, taking hold of Henry's and Tyler's shirts and pulling them back. "What the heck is that?"

"An area depleted of oxygen, unable to support life." He gets up, takes a small book from his other pocket. It says *Field Guide to Southern Wisconsin* on the cover. He opens it to a page with the corner folded over.

I swallow. "What do you mean exactly, 'unable to support life'?"

The boy runs his finger down the page, then closes the book. "I think that's pretty self-explanatory." He slides the magnifying glass and book back into his pocket, then picks up a long stick from the ground. He dips it into the water and lifts it out. The stick has a green tinge.

"Well, that settles one question. It's not filamentous. You'd see long pieces attached."

Maya stares at him. "What?"

"I'm very sorry to say that it looks like things are happening here. Bad things."

I feel a flutter in my chest.

"You mean bad guys?" Henry shouts. "Like Darth Vader?" He tries to poke his lightsaber into the lake but Maya stops him again.

The boy squints at us. "I need to go look something up. I don't have a signal out here." He turns away and starts walking down the shore. His shoelaces are untied and flapping on the ground.

"Just a second!" I call. "What are you talking about? What kind of bad things?" The boy doesn't stop or look back.

"Weirdo," Tyler says.

"You don't get to call him a weirdo," Henry replies. "I do. Weirdo."

The boy zigzags through blankets and chairs, then heads toward the cabins. He must be staying in one of them.

"That guy is completely, one hundred percent creepy, trying to scare us like that," Maya says. "Nice act, with the magnifying glass. Dead zone, gimme a break. That's right out of a horror movie." She nudges me. "Don'tcha think?"

"Maybe . . . I don't know. . . ."

"Wait, you believe what he said?"

"Well, he seemed to know what he was talking about, with the algae and the filamen—whatever."

"Annalise, it's probably just lake gunk. Or maybe someone poured something into the water. Who knows. I'm sure it'll go away."

Henry and Tyler tug on Maya's hands, chanting "We want a snack! We want a snack!" They race each other to the blanket and Maya tears after them, calling over her shoulder, "Text you later if I'm still alive!"

I look at the green coating and my heart flutters again. It seems plastered to the surface. Lake gunk? Something about it doesn't feel right.

Chapter Eight

RENN

There are a couple of cigarette butts, several brightly colored cans, and a jagged metal piece rolling about in Tru's waters. A shopping cart is lying on its side, two wheels spinning in the wind.

My cousin catapults a can into the air. It sails a long distance, lands in me with a plunk, then floats aimlessly. Normally, I would be mad—that wasn't very nice—but I don't have enough energy to be mad.

Tru's been in moods a lot lately. I try calling out. Doubt I'll get an answer. Tru never was much of a talker, or a listener. More of a foot-stomper, like Annalise's sister. But I hear a rumble.

"Tru?" I say again.

Another rumble, then a sort of growl. "What?"

"I wanted to ask you something."

"Ask."

"Remember when we were little?"

"What about it?"

"When it was different here. When we were different."

Tru glares at the shopping cart. "I remember."

"When boats didn't have grimy engines that spit out gas and oil. When Marked Tree Trail was the way people went places, not speeding cars down rows of asphalt." My water feels heavy. Still, and warm. No breeze today. "Asphalt is not our friend, Tru. And neither is all this rain. Too many storms."

My cousin slaps her bank. "No use looking back. Things change. This is the way it is now. People's hearts have gone sour."

I think of Annalise. "There are still good hearts."

"Can't say I agree." Tru thrashes for a while, then quiets to a gray rippling. "Remember that game we used to play? With the fish?"

I part my water into a slow smile. "Who has more?"

Tru smiles too. "Who has more fish? I always won."

"You're longer. Wasn't really a fair matchup. But it was fun to try to count them." I picture the dead, young fish. "Sometimes, I can't breathe right. Not enough air. Do you ever feel that way, Tru?"

"Sometimes."

It's as though my heart is being smashed, pushed deep down to the layers of sediment at the bottom. "What's happening to us?" I ask softly.

Tru becomes as motionless as the solid rock beneath us. "I'm not sure, Renn. But I don't think things will ever go back to the way they were when we were little."

Algae has been around forever. But not like this. Closed-up and dark and oozing. Mean around the edges. A musty odor. When I try to shift it, break it apart, it doesn't budge. Like what people use to repair things at the canoe tent. Glue. That word doesn't bounce or echo, it sticks.

"Remember," I whisper to Tru. "Remember when we were looked after? When we were really loved?"

Tru doesn't answer.

Chapter Nine

ANNALISE

I bend toward the water and look closer. The start of a dead zone? Was that boy trying to scare us, like Maya said? Or does he really know what's happening? I spot another dead fish, floating on its side. There are clumps of green on its silver scales, more than the last one had.

I walk away from the reeds and kneel by a clearer part of the water. "Renn? Everything okay?"

There's a pause, then: *I've been better.*

"What's wrong?"

Hard to explain.

"Do you feel sick?"

A little.

I dip my hand in. "You're warm. When people's foreheads are warm, they have a fever. Maybe you have a fever. Can that happen to a lake? Maybe you need, like, medicine?"

Maybe.

Renn is very still. I don't see any ripples or waves. "That green stuff over there . . . do you know what it is?"

Some kind of algae. A bloom, I think.

"Is that where you feel sick?"

Yes.

"Has this ever happened before?"

I barely hear the answer. It's just a tremble, really.

No. Not like this.

I stand, getting a glimpse of the dead fish again. Did it swallow the algae and choke? Or was it trapped and couldn't swim away? My stomach rolls over. I need to find Dad. And I need to find that boy.

I rush toward the office, stepping around blankets and coolers and people. When I get there, Mom's straightening up the front desk while Jess is reading aloud from a piece of paper.

"Option one: I can take a bus. I checked it out. The driver will watch a younger kid. I'll sit in the first seat. It's only, like, twenty bucks, and it'll take me to downtown Madison, a couple of blocks from the audition. I can take the bus right back afterward. Option two: Amy's mom can drive me and bring me home. They said it's okay. Option three—"

"Who's Amy?" I interrupt.

"My best friend. She wants to be an actor too."

"I thought Emily was your best friend," I say.

"Oh, we're not friends anymore."

Mom stops, puts down a stack of brochures. "Really? Since when?"

"Since the last day of school when she told everybody not to be friends with me anymore. But Amy didn't listen. So we're BFFs now."

"You didn't tell me," Mom says. "What happened?"

Jess rolls her eyes. "Long story. There was a whole big scene at the three-legged race during the class party. Actually, not so long. Emily turned into a mean girl."

Mom sighs. "Are you okay?"

She shrugs. "Yeah. I don't want to be friends with her either."

Mom puts a rubber band around the brochures. "Jess . . . I don't know Amy's mom, and I told you how busy we are right now, plus everything we talked about with you starting things, and then—"

"You don't have to worry. Her mom's super nice."

I butt in. "Where's Dad?"

"He went to get a part for the vacuum," Mom answers. "It's not working."

"So, which option?" Jess asks.

An older man and woman come in, asking for restaurant recommendations. Mom mentions a few places, showing them a binder with menus that we keep at the front desk.

While she's talking to them, I glance at the Thought Wall. More notes are tacked up: *I flunked art. Ice cream makes everything better. Carly F likes Dylan G. If Cinderella's shoe fit, then why did it fall off?*

The couple asks if they can borrow the binder, and Mom says "Of course." They take it outside and sit at one of the picnic tables.

I glance out at Renn. I don't see any green from where I'm standing. It seems to be only down by the reeds, which makes me feel a little better. "Mom, can you tell Dad I need to talk to him when he gets back? I think something might be going on with the lake."

"Who cares about some lake in the middle of nowhere!" Jess snaps.

"Um, I do."

"Sure," Mom says to me, then looks at Jess. "The yelling needs to stop. Dad and I will discuss it, but *no promises.* Understand? And I want to see all the information about the audition."

"Done!" Jess tears out of the office and runs toward the water. I see her pick up a stone and throw it. An amazingly good throw, actually, for someone so small. It lands with a splash and Renn gobbles it up. Jess stands there, hands on hips, her back to the cabins.

Mom opens her laptop and sips her coffee. "This was warm at some point."

"You need me to do anything?"

"Not right now. I have to catch up on emails."

I walk outside, looking for the boy. Finally, I see him near the canoe tent, inspecting the bottom of a canoe with his magnifying glass. Does he carry that around with him all the time?

I jog over. I clear my throat, but he doesn't look up. "Um, excuse me."

Still stooped over, he peers up at me through the glass, which makes his eye enormous. It's dark brown, the color of soil.

"Hi, I'm Annalise. My parents own the cabins."

He lowers the glass, straightens up. "Zach."

His shorts and shirt droop off him like they're on a hanger. "You were just looking at that green stuff. The algae?"

"Yeah?"

"Well, how do you know it could be the start of a dead zone?"

He opens his book and taps a picture. It's a lake with a green coating—similar to the one by the reeds, except much bigger—covering most of the surface.

"Blue-green algae," he says. "Technically, cyanobacteria. This is an algal bloom."

My mouth gets dry. *A bloom?* That's what Renn said.

Zach closes the book. "We learned about these in

science last year. Never thought I'd see one up close, though."

"But this isn't like that. In the picture, the bloom is huge. Here, it's just one little area, if that's what it is. The rest of the lake is fine."

"For the moment." Suddenly, Zach starts blinking crazily, covering one eye with a hand. "Not again," he groans, then peels something from his eye. "I just got contacts. I'm failing miserably at keeping them in. I suspect my corneas are rejecting the foreign objects." He walks away, stumbling a little.

"Wait, where are you going?"

"To get my glasses."

I follow him to cabin 8. He takes a key from his pocket and opens the door.

"Oh, you're staying in this cabin?"

He gives me a little smile. "No, I stole the key from the front desk." He disappears inside and comes back out a minute later, wearing glasses with square black frames. "I'm here for a month with my dad. He thinks this is the perfect place to finally write his novel. We arrived two days ago and he's been staring at a blank screen ever since. So, you know, lots of progress."

"Where do you live?"

"Chicago."

He takes off the glasses and cleans them on his shirt, then slides them back on. I bet Zach's really bored and he's pranking us, like we're dumb small-town kids.

I cross my arms. "I don't believe you. The bloom—or whatever it is—will evaporate or sink or go away on its own in a few days, and the lake will be fine."

He shakes his head slowly.

"I'm sure it's not bacteria. Something probably just got in the water."

"Cyanobacteria."

"Okay, cyanobacteria. *Our* lake, *my* lake, doesn't have that."

He doesn't reply, but walks toward a picnic table, then grabs a clear plastic cup someone left behind. He heads to the water.

I run after him. "What are you doing?"

"There's something else I want to check."

I follow him down the shore to the reeds. Zach kneels, holds the cup with the edges of his fingers, then drags it through the gunk. He places the cup on the ground.

"What are you checking?"

"I'm looking for an indicator. The contents need to settle."

The slimy liquid swirls slowly in the cup. "So the bacteria's going to magically appear?"

"Sort of."

I glance at him. "Do you want to be a scientist or something?"

He shrugs. "Maybe. What about you?"

"Possibly something to do with bedding."

"Bedding?"

I sigh. "Never mind."

We sit in silence for a few minutes. Tiny green flecks start to emerge in the water inside the cup. Sort of like floating particles of dust. Zach lifts the cup, holds it in front of his face and turns it around.

I stare at the little bit of Renn, trapped in the plastic. Suddenly, it doesn't seem like Zach's making this up or pranking us. Something did appear.

He puts the cup down next to me. "I'm sorry."

"This is bad?"

"I mean, it's just a jar test, but . . ."

"But what?"

"It could be very bad."

"But I'm sure there's a way to clean this up."

"From what I remember, there isn't an easy solution."

His shoelaces are still untied. One of them has a spilled drop of the greenish water. "You learned all this in science? Are you in high school?"

"Next year. I just finished eighth." He pulls out his phone, looks at it, then shoves it back into his pocket.

"You must miss your friends. And you won't see them for a whole month."

"Oh, yeah, for sure. We've been texting nonstop." He stands, brushes off his shorts. "Well . . . my dad's probably wondering where I am. I should go."

He walks toward the cabins. I glance at the cup, then at the reeds. It's so . . . quiet. Not like in winter, when the surface of the lake is covered with ice and snow. That's a restful, peaceful quiet. Even though I miss talking and listening, I know Renn is hibernating during those months. This is different. This feels like the kind of quiet where no one knows what to say.

"Renn?" I ask.

A murmur comes from the clear water, where the bloom ends. I go over there. "Don't worry. We'll clean this up, or get medicine, whatever you need." I sit, draw up my legs. "I promise."

Another murmur. Then a soft, weak *Thank you.*

I think about how I wore that armor hat with the pom-pom and tassels every day for almost a year. Then, one boiling hot summer afternoon when Mom, Dad, Jess, and I were at the Milwaukee Zoo, I took it off. We were eating lunch and my head was unbearably sweaty and itchy. I put it on the bench. As we were leaving to go to the reptile house, I forgot to take it. We went back, but it was gone. I looked at every single kid walking around the zoo but didn't see anyone wearing my hat. When we got back to the cabins, I ran out to Renn and sobbed as I told the story. "What's going to protect me now?" I wailed.

And Renn said, *I will.*

Chapter Ten

RENN

Night.

Frog melodies blend with the hums of the cicadas, crickets, and katydids. The moon shimmers across me. Now and then, there's the splash of a restless fish.

I cannot sleep.

Funny thing. When people are around, I yearn for a break from the noise. But when they're gone, I count the slow, long hours until morning when they return.

I pass the time by sifting through their lost possessions. I have quite a collection at the bottom. Keys, sunglasses, fossils, and canoe paddles, as I mentioned.

Also:

One rusty hammer.

Seventeen phones.

Two skateboards.

Thirty-nine shoes.

Forty-seven hats.

Glass bottles of all shapes and sizes, too many to count.

Plastic forks and knives and spoons.

Gold rings. Silver ones too.

One chair.

One microwave oven.

Two umbrellas.

Books. Bits of fibers that once were books.

Golf balls, footballs, baseballs.

And a gazing ball, like in the Alden's window. I brush away some mud and examine the red-silver-purple swirls in the glass. If I gaze at it, maybe it can tell me something about the strange algae. I try, but the ball shows nothing.

The night inches on. The insects become a low buzz. The fish settle. And I grow weary, sifting and counting.

Toward dawn, I feel worse. Perhaps it is a fever, like Annalise said, and I do need medicine.

The sun pokes its rays over the roofs of the cabins and the birds begin to chirp. The lindens and pines rustle and yawn and stretch their network of roots. Tru, surprisingly, sends me a playful wave. But I am too tired, too sluggish, to reply.

Chapter Eleven

ANNALISE

Mom and Dad get home late. As soon as they pull into the driveway, Jess leaps from the porch swing where she's been waiting. "Whenever you're ready, I can show you everything about the audition!"

Mom climbs the steps slowly, gripping the railing. "Okay, let's get something to eat. It's been a long day."

"I need to talk to you guys too," I say. "It's important."

Jess rushes past me, following Mom and Dad to the kitchen. "I'm first!"

Dad takes a container from the fridge. "Leftover mac 'n' cheese?"

"Fine," Mom says. "Did you two eat?"

Jess pulls out a chair. "We made sandwiches."

Dad puts the food in the microwave and then sits next to Jess. "Let's see what this is all about." She hands him her phone.

Dad scrolls down. "Cucumber Productions? That's who's making the movie?"

Jess nods. "Indie film."

"Hmm. There's an audition fee? Fifteen dollars. Is that standard?"

"I'm sure that's normal. I mean, they have a lot of costs, right? It's expensive to make a movie. You have the director, all the actors, the set . . ." Her voice trails off as Dad keeps scrolling, frowning a little.

The microwave beeps and Mom takes out the bowl. "It could be a scam, Jess. What do we know about this production company just by looking at their website?"

"It's not a scam. I checked it out."

Dad gives Jess her phone, and glances at Mom as she brings two forks, dishes, and the bowl to the table. They're not saying anything.

Jess looks from one to the other. "You've already made up your mind. You're going to say no, aren't you?"

"I know I asked you to show me the information," Mom starts, eyeing Dad.

"We did discuss it," he continues, "but we think it's better if you try out for something here—"

Jess jumps up, then runs upstairs, sobbing. Her door slams, echoing through the house.

Mom picks at the macaroni.

Dad sighs. "What did you want to talk about, Annalise?"

I tell them about Zach and the algae. "He's staying in cabin eight with his dad. He dipped a cup into the lake out by the reeds and there were, like, little green specks in the water. He said it's bad, and there's bacteria, and it could turn into a dead zone."

Dad says, "Hmm. It's too dark to see anything now, but I'll take a look first thing in the morning. It's by the cove?"

"Yeah, you'll see the cup. Thanks. It's really scaring me."

"I wouldn't worry too much. Algae's common in lakes. Part of the ecosystem. It comes and goes, and only some species are harmful. They came out and tested for E. coli a week ago and the report was negative. I know some lakes have had problems with algae recently, but like my father always used to say, 'Panic only when necessary.' "

I blow out a long breath. "Okay. I'll try not to panic."

"Jay," Mom says softly, putting her fork down. "Maybe we should let her go to the audition."

"No. We made our decision. It's too much right now."

"It's just, she's so excited, and something happened with her friends . . ."

"This thing doesn't even sound legit, Jackie. She

always nags us until we give in. She can find something else." He changes the subject and starts telling Mom about the vacuum, which sounds like it can't be repaired.

"If we're going to pay for roof and window repairs, let's use our own vacuum for now," Mom says. "We'll deal with getting a new one later."

"Okay." Dad brings his dish to the sink. "You know, I was thinking. Since we're full up, what about bringing back those activities we used to do years ago when every cabin was booked all summer long? Marshmallow roasts, ghost story night, movies under the stars."

Mom nods. "Great idea. I always loved those."

"But is that stuff too corny now? Annalise, do you think kids would still be into it?"

"Those things never get old," I say.

Dad grins. "Good answer."

They start rinsing the dishes and I go upstairs, still worrying about the algae. Renn's voice didn't sound like it usually does. But Dad has to be right. He knows a lot more than Zach, who's only studied lakes in science class.

One of the pictures in my frame is a snow-covered Renn. When the ice and snow start melting at the end of winter, I can't wait for Renn to wake up. The first winter, when I was three, I didn't understand why I couldn't hear anything. I asked Mom why the lake couldn't talk. She smiled and told me that nature takes a long sleep to store up energy for spring and summer. When I finally saw some ripples that next April, I splashed my hand in the chilly water and told Renn everything I'd done over the winter. And Renn said, *I missed you too.*

I get the jar from my dresser and drop in a penny I found by the soda machine. I'm hoping it's good luck and the algae will turn out to be nothing. I rotate the jar, then give it a shake, admiring the delicious weight of all the coins.

"Where'd you get all that money?"

I jump. Jess is leaning against my doorframe. "From the cabins."

"So technically, it isn't really yours."

"Um, no, it is. People lost them. I found them."

"What are you gonna use it for?"

"I'm not sure."

"How much do you have?"

"Why do you want to know?"

She picks at her nail polish. A few green flakes flutter to the floor. "No reason. Just curious."

"Jess . . . I *know* you have a reason. Tell me."

"I don't! I was just asking." Foot stomp. "And it's JessiKa! Why is no one calling me that?" She dashes down the hall. Door slam, again.

I start to put the jar back on my dresser, then change my mind. I stick it behind a pair of boots on my closet floor. Not that I don't trust Jess . . . but my sister doesn't react well to being told no.

When she was in second grade, she begged Mom and Dad to get her a pet frog, but they said she was too young to take care of a pet herself. So she went to the lake, plucked one from the water, and brought it home. Dad lectured her as they went back and returned it. Last year, Jess wanted to get hair extensions but that was a no too. She used clear tape, the kind for boxes, to attach two imitation blond braids to her hair. Mom had to cut them out. Her hair is still growing back.

What is my sister going to come up with now?

The next morning when I wake up, there's no sound from Jess's room and her door is still closed. Mom and Dad are already gone. They leave before six every day in the summer. I figure Jess will sulk for a while, so I don't call her. I grab my cap and a granola bar and start walking to the cabins.

Main is quiet, the shops aren't open yet. The flamingos are upright in the Alden's window, and one is wiggling a little. Mr. Alden is there, trying to position it. I stop as he looks at me and holds up a hand. His palm has worn lines, like the grooves on a seashell. I start to raise my hand too because I know I should, but it falters and drops loosely to my side. Does he know that Mrs. Alden was in the window on my found days?

A little ping plucks my heart as he keeps attempting to steady the flamingo. I didn't go to the funeral. Or to their house afterward. Mom and Dad didn't make me. They let me decide. I went to Maya's house that day and played with her new kitten.

Maya's parents went. Everyone in town did, I think. The cemetery's off the highway, on a hill as you leave town. Mom's family is buried there. Every time I pictured people in black gathered around Mrs. Alden's casket, dabbing their eyes, I stroked the kitten's soft fur and held him close to my chest. Maya offered to let me take him home for the night. "He could have a sleepover at your house," she said. I told her thanks, but I was okay, I really was. Besides, Jess is allergic to cats.

A breeze tumbles a crumpled newspaper page across the sidewalk until it gets wrapped around a lamppost. I stare at the row of flamingos, ALDEN'S GIFTS stamped on all of their necks. Like they're the property of the store. Like I was.

They called me the "Alden's Baby" during the police investigation, in the news stories, and on the flyers.

No clues emerge in mysterious Alden's Baby case.

Officials search for Alden's Baby witnesses.

Phone tip line set up for Alden's Baby probe.

Alden's Baby investigation at a standstill.

What was the person thinking, dumping me *here*? Not at a fire station, not at a hospital. Who would do that to their *child*?

The day of Mrs. Alden's funeral, after I left Maya's, I found a small, corked glass bottle with layers of colored sand floating in the lake. A kid must have made it, then lost it. I fished the bottle out, and held it up, the colors glinting in the sun.

"How did this end up here?" I asked.

Renn took a moment to answer. *How do things end up anywhere?*

Mr. Alden isn't in the window anymore. The door creaks, starts to open.

I yank the Renn Lake Rentals cap down so low it practically covers my eyes, then run.

I could find my way there with a blindfold on. In the middle of the night. With every step, every slap of my soles on the sidewalk, I feel like I'm pushing away the Alden's Baby. And when I get to the water, that unknown baby evaporates. I'm me, not her, and I have a name.

Chapter Twelve

RENN

I feel the muffled vibrations of people moving around me. I hear fragments of words, but it's like they're high up, wrapped inside a cloud. I smell sharps and sweets, sours and acids.

The bloom. It's gotten bigger.

I sense the pulsing of the trees, whispering to each other through their roots.

But I cannot see them, or the people.

And my waters are completely . . .

Silent.

Chapter Thirteen

ANNALISE

I reach the shore, and I'm about to look for a quiet spot to talk to Renn, but a crowd is gathered. Kids and adults, pointing and talking and pacing back and forth. No one's in the lake. Maya's there, holding Henry's and Tyler's hands, and so is Dad, standing next to . . . Zach? Zach's showing him something in his book.

I weave through the crowd.

"Annalise." Dad's face is crumpled.

"What's happening? Why's everyone—"

He gestures to the water. I move closer and see a long, wide patch of the same kind of thick algae that was by the reeds but is now near the shore and all around the pier. It goes out to about the middle of the lake. On the far side, by the other shore, I glimpse Renn's water mirroring the sky. Glassy and quiet. Too still.

Dad comes up next to me. "I'm afraid this must've

blown in overnight from that area you told me about." His voice is scratchy. "I know that can happen."

"Looks like a HAB." Zach is suddenly at our side, blinking rapidly and rubbing one eye.

My throat gets an instant lump. "What's that?"

"A harmful algal bloom," Dad says quietly. "But we don't know if that's what this is."

People are circling around the matted green patch and it's making me dizzy. "There was only that little part yesterday. I don't understand. How did it get this big? You said the E. coli report was negative."

Dad sighs. "Different thing."

"Were there some bad storms recently?" Zach asks.

"Yes," I say. "There've been a lot, actually."

"Runoff," Zach nods. "After a lot of rain, debris gets carried into the lake."

"That's right," Dad says. "Unfortunately, all kinds of pollutants can wind up in our lake, like fertilizer from farms, pesticides, household chemicals, even pet waste. Then there's too much nitrogen and phosphorus in the water, and if it's warm, the conditions are ripe for a bloom."

"You can't see it growing," Zach adds. "Cyanobacteria are microscopic."

Dad takes out his phone. "This has to be reported.

Probably tested. I need to call the health department." He walks away, tapping his screen.

"Even though it seems like this happened overnight, it's been building for a while," Zach says. He picks up a pebble and tosses it onto the algae. It sits on top, caught.

I hear Dad talking on the phone.

"Leo and I did a project together in science about . . ." Zach picks up another pebble but doesn't throw it. He rolls it between his fingers.

"About algae?"

"No," Zach says quickly, letting the pebble drop. "Nothing. Forget it."

"Annalise!" Maya's walking toward us, with Henry and Tyler. "I texted you. Why don't you check your phone like a normal person?"

"Oh, sorry . . ." I don't even remember hearing it buzz.

Henry jabs Zach's leg with his lightsaber. "Hey, kid!"

"Excuse me." Maya taps Henry's shoulder. "We do not attack people like they do in video games. This is real life."

Henry rolls his eyes, then turns to Zach. "I looked up 'dead zone' last night on my tablet. This bacteria's, like, the worst, most powerful, evil force in the universe. And it's invisible!"

"That's about right," Zach says.

Henry flips on his lightsaber and lifts it into the air. "But I'm gonna destroy it!"

"What's your plan?" Maya asks, smiling.

"I'm gonna shred it, rip it apart, blow it up!" He makes an explosion sound.

"Me too!" Tyler says, turning on his lightsaber and waving it around. "Hi-ya!"

"If only," Zach says.

My mouth feels dry and chalky. Questions are bouncing around in my head but can't make their way out.

Tyler jumps up and down. "Henry! Isn't the color like the Hulk?"

"Yeah!" They slap their palms in a high five.

Dad says, "Okay, thank you. I'll spread the word." He hangs up, then claps. "Attention, everyone! Until the health department can get here, we're to stay out of the water. I'm going to put up a sign. I'm sure they'll take care of it soon. We'll get this under control, folks; no need to be alarmed."

"This looks so gross," Maya says. "A total oy vey! Who'd even want to go in the water?" She takes a picture of the lake with her phone.

Henry and Tyler run around, flipping their lightsabers on and off, yelling that nobody should move and they're going to get the bacteria before it gets us.

Maya looks at Zach. "We haven't exactly met. I'm Maya. Helping my crazy aunt bring back Yiddish, one *oy vey* at a time."

He laughs. "Hi. Zach."

"You're staying at the cabins?"

He nods. "With my dad. The novelist." He rolls his eyes.

"What's he written?"

"Ten pages."

"Oh. Cool, though, that he's trying."

Zach shrugs.

"Anyway," she says, "I'm sure the health department will know what to do. They must have a machine or something to get the algae off. Or, like, dissolve it?"

"The thing is, if you skim a bloom, you could spread the toxic bacteria, make it worse. It's not a quick fix."

She tilts her head. "Toxic bacteria? Okay, science is my worst subject, but I don't think you should go around saying that before we know if it's true. You'll scare people."

Maya's using her class president voice. Last year, she started the RL Café at school—a place we could hang out on Friday nights. She raised money, planned the once-a-month events, and oversaw a committee. Everyone loved them, even though they grumbled that Maya was bossy about every single detail.

Zach peels off his contacts and squints at the water. "I was just trying to help."

"Yeah, I get that. And thanks. But let's just see what they say."

I can't listen anymore. I walk away from them, and all the people who are murmuring and talking to Dad. Everything blurs into the background as I go as close as possible to the lake without touching the algae. Seeing the green pierces my heart and makes my head hurt.

I remember so clearly the first time I heard Renn. I wasn't startled. It seemed perfectly normal that I could hear a lake. As I got older, I knew it wasn't exactly normal. I didn't tell anyone that I still talked to Renn. Would the magic stop if my secret was let out into the world and I tried to explain it to Mom or Dad or Jess, or even Maya? No, this was something to keep private.

I kneel down, whisper. "Renn."

No answer.

"Renn?" I say a little louder, my heart pounding.

Nothing.

"Can you hear me?"

An awful, deafening, terrifying . . .

Silence.

Chapter Fourteen

RENN

Terrible words are hovering, hanging by their necks in the air above me.

They drop down and stick to me, like the algae.

I hear Annalise call.

I try, but I am unable to answer.

Chapter Fifteen

ANNALISE

Why can't I hear Renn?

Has the bloom affected Renn's voice?

Zach's words come rushing back to me: *Unable to support life.* Dad said we have to stay out of the water. But what about the fish, and the turtles and frogs? How can they stay out of the water?

Something touches the edge of my shoe and I look down. It's a key, attached to a flat metal circle. Faded letters are etched in script on the circle: RENN LAKE RENTALS. We don't have keys like this anymore. It must've been dropped into the water a long time ago. The room number on the key is hard to make out; there are just two curved lines left.

This isn't a coincidence. Renn sent me the key. Just like the arrowhead. But why?

The key and the metal piece have specks of green. I probably shouldn't touch them. I hunt for something to wipe them off with and grab some leaves. I make a sandwich with the key between the leaves and pick it up carefully. I'll clean the key at the office.

I repeat what I told Renn yesterday. "Don't worry," I whisper. "We'll do whatever we can to make you better. I promise."

No reply, not even a ripple.

There's a group of people surrounding Dad, firing questions at him.

"When will they inspect the water?"

"What do they think it is?"

"This is our vacation. What are we supposed to do if we can't use the lake?"

"My son was in the lake yesterday! I mean, he showered off, but—"

"So was my daughter! Should we be worried?"

Dad's face is even more crumpled. They're not letting him answer.

I walk toward Maya, who's loading things into her backpack. "I guess we're not going to hang out here today," she says. "You guys want to go to the park?"

Tyler shrugs. "Yeah. Okay."

Henry groans. "The park is boring."

"Not today." Maya puts a finger over her lips. "I heard there's buried treasure."

Tyler's mouth drops open, but Henry narrows his eyes. "Really? Who told you that?"

"It's a secret legend. Not that many people know about it." Maya elbows me, then whispers, "I think I'm getting this whole babysitter thing. You just have to make stuff up." She shakes her phone. "By the way, this is a convenient device for keeping in touch with your best friend when you're not with her."

I smile.

She hugs me. "It'll be fine."

"I hope so."

She grins at me. "Blimperfly!"

"Yeah . . . I know . . ."

"Okay, I can't believe I'm actually going to quote my parents, but here goes: 'There isn't a problem that can't be solved.'"

"Aren't they usually referring to cavities?"

Maya holds out her palms and raises them up and down. "Cavities, lake. A problem's a problem. Am I right?"

"C'mon, Maya." Tyler tugs her shorts. "I want to look for the treasure."

She picks up her backpack. "Let me know if anything else happens. Like, you know, a gruesome swamp creature rises from the water."

"Not funny," I say.

She slings her backpack over one shoulder. "Hey, wanna help me put up posters for the Fourth of July Fest? It'll cheer you up."

"Now?"

"No, whenever my parents get them back from the printer. You know they're chairing the fest this year?"

"Yeah, sure . . ."

Henry sprints ahead, yelling for Maya to hurry. Tyler barrels after him. Maya waves to me, then races to catch up. "Wait for me, please!"

Holding the leaf-key sandwich gingerly, I head toward the office. Zach slips out from behind a tree and falls into step with me. He's wearing his glasses.

He looks at the ground as we walk. "I just wanted to say I'm sorry about all this."

"It's not your fault." I sigh, glance at him. "Did you give up on the contacts?"

"No. Not yet."

"Why do you want them? They don't seem to be working out very well."

"I thought when I start high school . . . forget it. It's stupid."

"I think you look fine in glasses. And they're cool. For a while, Maya was wearing glasses even though she didn't need them."

He shrugs, points to the leaves. "What's that?"

"An old key washed up." I carefully take off the top leaf and show him.

"Now, that's cool. I love stuff like that. My dad has hundreds of old record albums. And matchbooks from restaurants. Sometimes, he takes them out and tells me stories about the places."

"Good to know he's not always inside a cabin." Zach's laces are loose again, and one still has that little green splotch. "So are untied shoes your signature look?" I joke.

"What's the point of tying them? They'll just untie."

"You could do double knots."

"The last thing I need in my life is more knots." He suddenly jogs toward his cabin. I call his name, but he quickly opens the door and disappears inside. What did I say?

Mom and Vera are in the office, going over the list of guests. Vera says "Hi," in a low, scratchy voice, then coughs.

"Good morning," Mom says. "Vera's still getting over that bad cold, so can you and Jess do the cabins today?"

My sister's rearranging the caps on the rack in rainbow order. She's wearing a sundress, a sequined headband, and long feather earrings.

"Sure. But did you hear what's happening with the lake?"

Mom nods sadly. "Dad texted me. And I saw it earlier. We'll see what they say."

I go into the office bathroom and wipe off the key with a wet paper towel. When it's clean and dry, I slide it into my pocket. I'll show Mom later at home. I motion to Jess. "Ready?"

She puts the last cap on the rack, then follows me to the supply closet. I hand her a stack of clean towels. "You're better?" I ask.

"I suppose I'll live."

"You'll find another audition."

She makes a pouty face. "For a movie being filmed in Wisconsin? Not likely."

We drag out the laundry bin and the vacuum. I knock on the first cabin. No answer. I knock again to make sure no one's there, then open the door with the office key.

Jess glances around the room. "Man, these people are messy."

There are clothes on the floor, towels piled on the bed, and several open boxes of crackers on the dresser, crumbs spilled everywhere. She gathers up the towels, then dumps them into the bin. I start making the bed while she vacuums, pretending she's dancing with it. I guess she will live.

We go from cabin to cabin, exchanging towels, changing sheets, straightening up. When we knock on the door to Zach's cabin, a man with stubble and dark circles under his eyes answers the door. He's wearing rumpled sweats and a stained T-shirt.

"Oh, hi," I say. "Do you want your room cleaned?"

He waves us away. "Not right now. I'm in the middle of something."

"Fresh towels?" Jess holds up a couple.

He takes them, says thanks, then shuts the door. Zach wasn't there.

As we're walking back to the office, Jess shades her eyes and looks out at the lake. "So what's going on? I got here late and missed all the commotion."

"See that green stuff on the surface?"

"Yeah."

I tell her what happened.

"Well"—she fingers one of the feather earrings—"maybe they can just, like, wash it off."

"Maybe. I hope so."

When we get inside, Sophie, the girl who was asking Dad about the dead fish, is standing by the Thought Wall with her grandparents. She's writing on a sticky note in crayon.

"You need help?" her grandma asks.

Sophie shakes her head and continues to write, biting

her lip. Then she gives the paper square to her grandma, who reads it, nods, then sticks it on the wall. I can see it clearly from where I'm standing.

The lake is sad, it says. Inside the *d,* she made a frowny face.

Her grandpa says, "C'mon, sweetheart," and takes her hand. They leave and I read those four words over and over. *The. Lake. Is. Sad.*

I pull the old, worn key from my pocket. In the dulled grooves, there's a green residue, like it's now permanent.

I go outside, walk across the empty shore, and try once more. "Renn?"

Nothing.

"Renn . . . why can't you . . ."

Then I understand. The two curved lines on the key . . . the old room number . . . it might've once been a six, but now, it looks like a broken heart.

Chapter Sixteen

RENN

Chapter Seventeen

ANNALISE

The next day, people from the health department come. They look important and official, with dark sunglasses and brown shirts tucked into khakis.

Two men and one woman talk to Dad and Greg, our mayor. They make notes on their clipboards and take pictures of the lake.

I stand close enough to overhear something about testing the water, how that's costly and they don't have enough staff, but then Greg says, "We can use our reserve fund to pay for the test. We need to know."

The woman gets tall rubber boots and long gloves from their truck, puts them on, and wades into the water. She dips glass vials into different areas of the algae, filling each to the top. One by one, she hands them to the men, who cork them tightly and label them with tape. Then they're arranged in a plastic holder with slots for each vial. It's all very precise and orderly.

A crowd slowly gathers. Maya, with Henry and Tyler, lightsabers in hands. Mom and Vera. Sophie and her grandparents. Some of the people who were shouting questions at Dad. Zach, with his glasses on, and even Jess. Everyone's watching.

The woman carefully lifts the vial holder and carries it to the truck. Pieces of Renn being taken away.

One of the men is talking to Dad. "The lab will analyze the samples for cyanobacteria. If that's positive, they'll test for toxins," he says.

"What's your gut feeling?" Dad asks, running a hand through his hair.

"Couldn't say. Only way to tell is to look at it under a microscope. There are hundreds of different algae species in Wisconsin. But we have been seeing blooms more frequently. Planktonic blue-green algae are what we're concerned about. That's your toxin producer."

Dad lowers his voice. "Do you think this is planktonic?"

The man looks at the algae. "We have to wait and see."

Dad nods. "Thank you."

"We'll be in touch as soon as possible. It'll take several days. Nothing to do now except sit tight. And stay out of the water." He gives Dad a nod as he leaves.

On the last day of school, my teacher handed everyone a roll of tape. She told us it was a funny kind of send-off, but it was to remind us that there'll be lots of times that something's torn, and the best thing to do is tape it back up and go on. I wish that I could tape up Renn right now and everything would be back to normal.

The other man pulls out Dad's cardboard, handwritten sign. He goes to their truck and comes back with an official sign, then shoves the metal pole into the dirt with several sharp smacks of a hammer.

HEALTH ALERT. TOXIC BLUE-GREEN ALGAE MAY BE PRESENT IN THIS AREA. AVOID SWALLOWING LAKE WATER AND DO NOT TOUCH ALGAL SCUMS. KEEP PETS AWAY FROM THE WATER. DO NOT SWIM IN AREAS WHERE YOU CANNOT SEE YOUR FEET IN KNEE-DEEP WATER.

There's a website at the bottom for more info, but I don't want to read any more right now. The sign is bad enough.

The people climb into their truck and drive away with the vials of Renn's broken heart sloshing around in the back.

Vera's talking to Mom. Maya's reading the sign to Henry and Tyler, who are insisting they can destroy the algae with their lightsabers. "Were you even listening," she asks, "it says 'do not touch'!" Jess is standing with a girl I don't recognize—is that Amy?—and they're both looking at their phones. Zach's leafing through his field guide.

I can barely look at the lake. My throat feels raw. My head's throbbing. I'm filled up with a heaviness, a dread, and it's heating up my skin, flowing into my muscles and bones.

A teenage boy with pimples and a big, bulging Adam's apple tosses a water bottle onto the algae. It sits on top of the scum, the plastic glinting in the sun. "Bull's-eye!" he shouts.

The boy next to him, short and muscular, is also holding a water bottle and he winds up to throw it too.

"Stop!" I yell, tearing toward them, pushing people out of the way.

The boy lowers his arm and looks at me like I'm crazy.

"Don't you dare throw that!" I yank the bottle from his hand. "Don't even *think* about it!"

"Hey," he says. "What's your problem?"

The boy with the pimples takes a step back. "Whoa. Chill, okay?"

I point the bottle at the two of them like it's a weapon. "Get away from the lake. Leave it alone."

The muscular boy shakes his head. "Are you, like, possessed or something?"

I shove the bottle closer to them and they laugh, put their hands up. "We surrender," one says. The other grins. “You gonna toss us in jail? Causing property damage with a water bottle?”

Mom comes up behind me and puts her hand on my shoulder. I’m shaking. I lower my arm and see that I’ve crushed the plastic. People are trying not to stare, but they are.

“Take it easy,” Mom says softly into my ear.

“No! I don’t want to take it easy.” I gulp and gesture to the water. “How can I take it easy?”

The two boys snort, slap each other’s backs, and jog down the shore.

Mom tucks a curl behind my ear. “We know, honey.”

But they don’t. None of them do.

How can Renn keep me safe when it’s sick, covered up, and silent? When parts of it have been taken away to a cold, sterile lab to be *analyzed*.

And when things are too close, too much, where do I go?

Chapter Eighteen

ANNALISE

Later that night, Mom, Dad, and I are sitting on the porch. I'm in the chair and Jess is on the steps, texting. Amy, probably. Mom and Dad are in the swing, Dad's long, thin fingers circled around Mom's hand. The only sound is the cicadas humming and buzzing.

I can tell Mom and Dad are trying not to look worried in front of us, but I overheard them while they cleaned up after dinner.

"What if people cancel their reservations?" Dad said in a soft voice. "The deposits are nonrefundable, but we'll be out a lot of money. Without the lake, there's not much to do around here. If we plan those marshmallow roasts and movies under the stars, will people still want to come?"

Mom sighed. "I read online that algal blooms are getting worse and there's more of them. I didn't think it could happen here."

They were quiet as dishes clinked and cabinets opened and closed. Their footsteps creaked on the old wood floor.

"We have some money saved up from snowplowing, don't we?" Mom asked.

Dad: "Not that much, to be honest. We spent a lot on those ads. Plus, we replaced every mattress last year. That wasn't cheap."

Mom: "Maybe we should put off the roof repairs until we hear from the health department. Or the new windows?"

Dad: "Maybe."

In the winter, when the cabins are closed, Mom and Dad run a snowplowing business. They've had some good customers—the urgent care clinic, the high school—but I know they're not sure who will still need them for the next season.

Jess shouts "Cool!" and breaks the silence on the porch. "Amy's going to do a song from *Hamilton* for her audition! She has an incredible voice. I'm sure they'll take her."

Mom nods. "I hope we can meet Amy soon. Invite her over?"

"Yeah, okay."

I take the broken-heart key out of my pocket. "I found this at the edge of the lake yesterday."

Mom reaches for the key. "Wow. I remember these from when I was a kid. How strange."

"I guess it just washed ashore."

"That's so random," Jess says, not looking up from her phone.

Mom traces the curved lines with her finger. "Hard to tell which cabin it was for."

"I thought six, maybe?"

"Could be." She puts the key on the table. "A memory of a different time, a different place. I wonder what Gramps did with all those old keys."

"What was it like?"

"Back then?" Mom closes her eyes. "Slower. Softer."

"Yes," Dad says, even though he didn't grow up here. Mom and Dad met in college. "Memories are like that."

"I vividly remember swimming in the lake when I was little," Mom says dreamily, touching her toes to the floor, gently rocking the swing. "The other side seemed a million miles away."

"Everything always looks so big when you're a kid," Dad says.

"I used to think that under the surface there was a magical land, filled with fairies and goblins. Water spirits. I'd search for them, keeping my eyes open underwater for as long as I could."

"Did you ever see one?" I ask.

She laughs. "Once, I was positive I saw a mermaid—I told everyone and they were all very amused—but I think it was just a large fish. I refused to believe that mermaids could only live in oceans."

"Hey, I *know* there are lake mermaids," Dad says. "I've read about them. They're rare, but they're out there."

Jess rolls her eyes and bumps down a step. *"Dad."*

Mom stops the swing with her foot. "I'm always so busy now. But there are times when I look out at the lake, and it's like I'm a kid and Gramps is in his shirt and suspenders behind the desk. Gram's baked a pie, and my dad is fixing something, whistling and talking to guests. I'm in the water, pushing myself deeper, hoping to spot a mermaid."

Dad pats her hand and we're quiet again. Even the cicadas seem to get quieter. Then a voice blasts from Jess's phone. "Hey! What's up, Oliver?"

I jump, and so does Mom.

"Hey, Miller!" Jess turns her phone toward us and I glimpse a girl on the screen with long brown hair. "This is Amy, everyone!" Jess says. "We have the same number of letters in our last names. So we're meant to be BFFs, right? She's going to do her audition song." Jess looks at the screen. "Okay, go."

Amy starts singing. She sounds pretty good but stops halfway through. "That's all I've practiced so far."

Jess claps. "That was completely amazing!"

Amy says thanks, then groans. "My dad is calling me." They tell each other goodbye about ten times until Jess finally puts her phone down.

I get a twinge of annoyance. "Aren't you worried about the lake? I can hardly think about anything else."

"Well, yeah. But other things are still going on. I'm helping her practice. This is important too."

"It's just a little audition. The algae, that could affect everything. I started reading about it online, and—"

"Hey!" Jess leaps up. "I'm trying to be a good friend!"

"I didn't say you weren't."

She slaps the railing. "It wasn't my fault that Emily fell into the mud at the class party and ruined her new skirt! She told everyone I pushed her because I wanted to win the race, but I didn't!"

"Oh, Jess," Mom says softly. "Are you sure you didn't push her?"

"I didn't! She cut in front of me and tripped. But no one saw. They all believed *her*!" She stomps her foot.

"Sounds like it was just a mix-up," I say. "Maybe you could explain—"

"Don't try to help, Annalise!"

Dad raises an eyebrow. "Jessica."

She huffs. "How come you never get mad at her? Of course you wouldn't!" Jess runs into the house and bangs up the stairs. A minute later, I hear her door slam.

Mom looks at Dad, then gets up. "I'll go talk to her." She goes inside.

It's just me and Dad, and the cicadas. I don't know what to say. Dad's quiet too. Finally, he leans forward and rests his elbows on his knees. "Everything will work out. Somehow."

I don't know if he means with Jess or the lake.

"Sometimes your sister reminds me of an excitable puppy, always getting into things and barking like crazy. You never know when she's going to nip your ankle."

"That felt like more than a nip."

"I don't think she meant it."

I sigh.

Dad clears his throat. "When we started the process to adopt you, it was complicated and stressful. We weren't sure if it was going to happen. I worried enough then to last me for the rest of my life. But"—he smiles—"here we are."

I blink back tears. What if the adoption hadn't happened? Sometimes I think about that in the dark, when I can't fall asleep. Where would I be?

"And the algae," Dad says. "It might look bad, but let's

not worry until we have to, okay? Maybe this'll turn out to be nothing. We're going to sit tight and wait for the results."

I wipe my eyes and nod. "Okay."

Dad stands, steadies the swing. "I'm beat. It's been a long day. You coming in?"

"In a minute."

He goes inside. I walk down the steps and park my bare feet in the grass. I listen for night sounds, but everything's still. It's like the whole of Renn Lake is holding its breath, waiting to see what the test shows. Even the moon seems dimmer.

I pick up the key from the table, then put it on the mantel next to the picture of Mom's family. I never knew her dad or grandfather. They were both gone before I was born. Sometimes I wonder what they'd think of me.

Something stirs from deep in my heart as I look at their faces, speckled with bits of sunlight through the tree branches. And I realize I know what I want to do when I grow up.

Jess figured it out a few days ago when we were on the porch and she was talking about living in LA. *I see how much you love them,* she said. *The cabins.*

Actually, I think I've known since the first time Renn said hello.

Chapter Nineteen

ANNALISE

The results are in, and it's bad.

The samples had toxins. High levels were in every vial.

Zach was right. It's a HAB, a harmful algal bloom.

What if the lake does become a dead zone? No mermaids could ever live there, not to mention fish and frogs and plants. And Renn . . .

Today, a different woman from the health department pulls out the sign and pounds a new one into the sandy dirt. It has a picture of a person swimming and a dog drinking lake water, and both have diagonal lines through them.

WARNING. AVOID CONTACT WITH
THE WATER.

TOXIC ALGAE PRESENT. LAKE
CONTAMINATED.

UNSAFE FOR PEOPLE AND PETS.

UNTIL FURTHER NOTICE: DO NOT SWIM.
DO NOT DRINK LAKE WATER. KEEP PETS
AWAY. AVOID AREAS OF SCUM.

CALL YOUR DOCTOR OR VETERINARIAN IF
YOU OR YOUR ANIMALS HAVE SUDDEN OR
UNEXPLAINED SICKNESS OR SIGNS
OF POISONING.

I read the words over and over but can barely process them. Just two keep echoing in my head: *Avoid Contact.*

I look at the water, more than half of it smothered with the toxic algae. I want to grab a canoe, furiously paddle out there, then do something, anything, so Renn can talk to me.

"I feel terrible about this." Behind me, Zach is poking the dirt with the toe of his shoe. Untied laces again. "I kept hoping it wasn't what I thought."

"I—I don't want to talk right now." I look away, but when I glance back, he's still there. "I just need to be by myself, okay?"

He doesn't move. "Are you all right?"

"Not really."

"Can I do anything?"

"Unless there's a solution in your book, probably not." I close my eyes for a second, try to feel any sort of sensation from Renn. Nothing. "This isn't just a lake to me. A body of water. See, I have this thing about it. . . ."

"What kind of thing?"

I take a deep breath and tell him about being abandoned at Alden's. The brief version. "But when I'm here, it's like . . ." I choke up, gaze toward Renn.

"It goes away," he says.

"Yes," I whisper. "And I can hear the lake. And it can hear me." I can't believe I said that to someone I barely know. The words just slipped out, like something was urging me to let him in. Trust him.

Zach sits on the ground, pulls up his legs, and wraps his arms around them. "That's astounding."

"But"—my voice cracks—"not anymore." I sit too. More like collapse. Under the weight of the glaring yellow, black, and red AVOID CONTACT sign.

"What did you used to hear?" he asks.

"It's hard to explain."

Zach takes off his glasses and rubs the sides of his nose. "Try me." He folds the glasses and puts them in his lap. His eyes look lonely and sad without them, and a little lost, like he can't focus.

"How the lake is feeling," I say. "And advice and comfort, when I'm upset."

"I love that. I can hear trees."

"You can?"

"Yes. Since I was little, and my parents split up." He

gestures toward the cabins. "I spend summers with my dad, but, well, he's always busy with something."

I nod.

"Anyway, that's when I started hearing trees. Some scientists think trees talk to each other through their roots."

"That's so cool."

"Yeah. Like how insects communicate with sounds and vibrations. Trees can warn each other when they're in danger. And they feel pain. They even know each other—there are parent trees, kids, aunts, and uncles." He stretches out his legs; I can see the outline of his knee-caps poking through his skin.

"Wow."

"I know, right? Incredible."

He puts his glasses back on. "Leo said he could hear trees too. I believed him at first."

"He was lying?"

"I think so. He said a lot of things."

We sit there, quiet for a few minutes. Zach fiddles with the bottom edge of his shirt. A spider scurries near my leg.

Zach clears his throat. "He broke up with me on February sixteenth. I didn't even see it coming. I got kind of messed up for a while, lost a lot of weight, felt like nothing mattered." He stares at the ground. "Everything I thought I knew about him was wrong. And the worst part? He found someone else, like, two weeks later."

"I'm really sorry."

"Then after the breakup, our group wasn't the same. It felt awkward, and weird. People sort of drifted to other friends. And I hid in my science notebooks. At least science makes sense. There are lots of days I'd take science over people."

He sighs. "My dad said I'll find someone else, but . . . it was hard to see Leo in the hall every day with . . . I was really glad when school was over." Zach swallows, tips his head toward the water. "So anyway, what are they going to do?"

"I don't know. They're holding a meeting tomorrow night at the library."

"Are you going?"

"Definitely."

"Can I go too, or is it just for people who live here?"

"I think anyone can come."

"Okay. I will."

I stand. "Well, I should probably get over to the office. Are you . . . better now?"

"Kinda." He gets up and turns the other way, toward Main, laces flapping.

"See ya later," I call. He holds up a hand as he's walking.

Inside the office, Dad's listening to a bunch of people, all wanting to know what's going to happen. Mom's on the phone, and every time she hangs up, it rings again. She keeps trying to explain that there's a meeting tomorrow and the lake will hopefully be back to normal very soon. But from what I can tell, some people are cancelling reservations. A woman standing near Dad says there are pictures of the lake on social media and she shows the crowd her phone. "That's the end of my vacation," she says, shaking her head.

Several Sharpies are on the floor by the Thought Wall. I pick them up, put them back into the cup, and straighten the stack of sticky notes. One note is on the table. I'm about to stick it onto the board, but it says: *Renn Lake stinks. Literally.*

I crush the small yellow square in my hand. I don't care about our Thought Wall rule, that anyone can write anything and it stays. I bury the paper in the wastebasket.

Maya bursts into the office with Henry and Tyler trailing behind. She drops onto the sofa under the window, then wipes her forehead with the top edge of her T-shirt. She digs in her backpack and throws a couple of bags of fruit snacks to the boys. They sit on the floor in front of her, rip them open, and start gobbling them up.

"Annalise." She motions, and I walk over. "What am I supposed to do with these two? Their attention span is four minutes, if I'm lucky. I was planning a lot of activities at the lake. But now—"

"Maya, forget about that. Did you see the new sign?"

"Yeah, I know, it's bad. But Annalise, I still have a job." She taps her phone screen. "I've started a list of other stuff we can do. The park *again,* the candy shop, a scavenger hunt, water balloons, an obstacle course. You have any more ideas?"

"No."

"Oh! We could cook, right?" She nudges Henry with her foot. "You guys like to cook? Like, pancakes? Cookies?"

"Yeah, sure," Henry says, crushing the fruit snack package.

"Maya! The lake is contaminated! Unsafe!" My voice is high-pitched and shaky.

She looks up. Tyler pulls her arm and she goes, "Shh. Not now." She stuffs her phone into her backpack.

"I looked online about harmful algal blooms," I say. "It's another problem related to climate change. They can last months and do a lot of damage."

Maya nods. "Listen, I was going to do it later after I drop off these two, but let's put up the fest posters around town. My dad just got them from the printer. What do you say? It'll take your mind off all this. You can't just sit around and be sad all day."

I grab a tissue from a box on the table. "Okay, but—"

"No buts." She raises an eyebrow at the boys. "You guys can help too."

Tyler claps. "My mom says I'm the best helper!"

I tell Dad where I'm going and he nods. People are still surrounding him, asking questions. "We'll have some other activities in the meantime. Who likes ghost stories?" Dad says, trying to sound enthusiastic. No one answers.

We walk to Maya's house, Henry and Tyler thrashing bushes and poking trees with their lightsabers. She goes inside and comes back out a minute later with a stack of posters and tape.

We're on our way back to Main when Maya says, "Last night, my parents were talking about how this is a big problem in other places too. They were on the phone with my grandpa in Florida, and he said there's a red tide and lots of dead fish right by his condo."

"Great. That isn't making me feel better."

"It doesn't mean that'll happen here."

"But it could."

"Let's not be all gloom and doom. They'll figure it out and everything will be fine. Come on, we've got work to do!" She sprints ahead and the boys run to catch up.

When we're in town, Maya hands me some posters and rattles off which stores I should go to. "We want them front and center in the windows. We'll have to share the tape. I only have one roll." She looks at Henry and Tyler. "You guys give us pieces of tape, okay? That's your job."

I've got the hardware store, the candy shop, and Alden's.

Maya starts to go toward the movie theater, then stops. "Do you want me to do Alden's?"

"No, no, it's okay. I can."

"Sure?"

"Uh-huh."

I poke my head inside the candy shop and the owner, Lorelei, reaches for the poster without my saying anything. She grins. "I was wondering when these were coming."

The glass case seems a little sparse. Not as much candy as usual. "I'll get the tape." I glance outside but don't see the boys.

"That's all right. I have some." Lorelei hangs the poster in the window.

"Thanks."

"Hope we get a big crowd this year."

"Yeah. Me too."

I walk out and look down the block. Mr. Alden is in front of the store, filling the water bowl for dogs. I tug down the cap, which I haven't taken off since found day, and force myself to go over there. He glances up as I get closer, but my steps are slowing.

Henry runs over and peels a couple of pieces of tape from his fingers and offers them to me. When I don't take them, he sticks them on my arm and dashes off.

Mr. Alden straightens up, placing a hand on his back. He gives me a soft smile. Just like Mrs. Alden did. Last year on found day, she was arranging roses in bud vases. She put a pink one up to her nose, then held it out toward me. I could almost smell it through the glass.

I stop a few feet away. All I can do is point to the window.

He comes toward me and reaches for the poster.

I pull off a piece of tape and stare at the fingerprints on it. When something bad happens, you can't always just tape it up like my teacher told us.

Trembling, I put the poster on a bench, then turn and fly across the street. Maya calls my name, but I don't stop until I get to the pier. I walk out a little. Green, everywhere. Renn, voiceless. Me, left with no one who can understand.

Chapter Twenty

ANNALISE

The next night, the library's meeting room is jammed with practically everyone in town. Mom and Dad are sitting in the first row with Greg, but I'm standing along the back wall. I see Zach at the opposite end, near the door. I'm surprised to see his dad next to him. I try to catch Zach's eye, but he's studying something in his field guide.

Jess insisted on going to Amy's house to help her prepare for the audition. Maya's not here either. She said she was too exhausted to get off the sofa, but I should let her know what happens.

The Main Street store owners are sitting together in the last row: Lorelei, George from the hardware store, and Jean from the movie theater, wearing her pink rhinestone cat's-eye glasses. Mr. Alden is in the middle of the row.

Jean pats his arm. "We all miss her. She was one

special lady, your Viv. Not a day goes by I don't think of her." Mr. Alden nods, and Jean hands him a tissue. He dabs his eyes.

A woman at the front of the room says, "Hello, everyone. Welcome." She's wearing a brown shirt and khakis, and a man in the same uniform is standing next to her.

She raises her hands. "If everyone could take a seat, or find a place to stand, and quiet down, please." Finally, the room settles.

"Thank you all for coming," she says. "I'm Kim Bajwa, from the county health department. We know how concerned you are. We are too. Water is our most precious resource and we take our lakes very seriously in Wisconsin.

"Algae is not a new issue, but we've been seeing an increase in the size and frequency of blooms. Polluted runoff is a cause, as well as our rising global temperatures. We work hard to monitor our lakes but, unfortunately, problems do occur."

She flips on the projector, taps a laptop keyboard, and a document appears on the whiteboard. "I'd like to share the results of the water-quality report."

There are lots of numbers, neatly displayed in columns and rows. I don't understand everything, but I get this: it's not great.

Kim explains the data, and after a while, people start

to shift in their seats. Mom and Dad are whispering to each other. Lorelei keeps shaking her head and elbowing George. Finally, Kim finishes. "My colleague Keith will explain further," she says.

Keith scans the room, stopping to rest his gaze every few seconds on someone's face. "Well, folks, I'll be honest, this isn't easy to deal with. While there are several treatments for harmful algal blooms, they're costly, may disrupt lake ecology, and usually aren't a permanent solution. And, treating the algae can cause more toxins to be released into the water, making the situation worse."

Now I catch Zach's eye. Exactly what he said and what I read online.

Keith adds, "There just aren't many good options for larger lakes."

Someone up front asks, "What do you suggest, then?"

"The best long-term approach to reducing or hopefully eliminating algal blooms is to make sure that phosphorous is prevented, or at least significantly reduced, from getting into the lake."

Long-term? Can Renn even breathe? How long is long-term?

Jean raises her hand, and Keith calls on her. "Could you explain what phosphorus is?"

"Sure. Phosphorus is an essential element for plant

and animal life, but when too much washes into the water, it can increase the chance a bloom will occur. Everything we do has an impact and can upset the balance. The problem starts in the land, not our water. Fertilizer, detergent, cleaning products, pesticides. Down the drain, the driveway, into the sewer. It all ends up in the lake—"

Dad interrupts. "But isn't there something that can be done right now?"

"We've consulted the Department of Natural Resources," Keith says. "Most of the treatments, such as pumping in air, circulating the water, or skimming the surface, were designed for ponds, not lakes. There are some new approaches being studied, but our recommendation is to wait for the bloom to dissipate on its own."

Wait? Not do anything?

My heart sinks, past my knees and my legs and my feet, into the floor of the library, into the earth below. Into the earth's crust, I think. Which must be cracking under all the bad stuff we're doing to it.

"How long will that take?" someone asks.

"Every situation is different," Keith replies. "A lot of factors come into play. Weeks, months, we don't know."

Several people jump from their chairs. Dad looks like he might cry. Mom can't seem to move. The shop owners murmur to each other: "My place was already skating on thin ice, now what's going to happen?" "I was counting on a busy summer. My shelves are stocked." "Mine too. I owe my vendors a lot of money."

Mom buries her face in her hands, then looks at Dad. "This feels as bad as the time a tornado damaged almost all of the cabins. I was little, but I remember we had no guests and there wasn't any money to pay for repairs, let alone groceries." She chokes up. "You know I stupidly asked if I could still get a birthday present?"

Dad pats her back. "You didn't know."

"Gramps almost sold the land. He got a terribly low offer, some fast-talking guy said he'd bail us out. I remember everyone argued. Gram wanted to sell. But in the end, Gramps said no. We rebuilt the cabins ourselves." She sniffles and tries to smile. "Maybe that's why the roofs and windows are falling apart."

Mr. Alden gets up slowly. The collar of his shirt is rumpled, and he has one sleeve rolled up, while the other is down and buttoned at his wrist. He's still wearing his wedding band. Lorelei hugs him. "How you holding up?" she asks.

"Some days good; other days, not so much," he answers.

"My husband's gone years now, and I still think of him

every day. It doesn't get easier, but it gets better," Lorelei says.

What Mom said . . . Mrs. Alden . . . *Wait* . . . Everything's swelling up inside me. I battle my way toward the door, brush past Zach, and finally tumble from the room.

"Annalise!" Zach comes after me.

I turn. "They're not going to do anything!"

"What can they do? It's complicated."

"Something! Can't they try one of those treatments? Maybe one would work. They're, like, giving up!"

"You heard what they said—"

"No!"

I bang open the library door and take off, sprinting madly down the streets. Park and Church and Main, up and down the blocks, until I finally stop in front of the candy shop and bend over, hands on my knees, breathing hard.

There's something leafy and coiled lying on the ground under a streetlamp. I look up. The long strand of ivy that was loose, dangling from the brick, hanging on for its life, fell off. It's alone.

A squeaky sound bubbles up in my throat. I swallow, try to soothe away the sudden scratchiness. I kneel, pick up the strand. The leaves are already becoming brittle, and one crumbles between my fingers.

I open my mouth, start to say something, to the ivy, to Renn, to myself . . . I don't know. But nothing comes out. I try again, but I've lost my voice too.

And then I know.

Renn is dying.

Chapter Twenty-One

TRU

I am boiling mad.

I'm having a tantru. Renn teased me that my outbursts weren't tantrums, but tan-*trus*.

I thrash about, throwing myself over my banks. I twist and whirl and swirl. I glare at the sun, at the earth, at the sky. I try to shove that shopping cart out from under me, but the thing won't budge. At least I've rusted the handle.

People. They're like the flies that constantly hover above my surface. I have no choice but to put up with both of them.

Most of my long, curving path from north to south is just me, coursing along, some parts high, other parts low. Miles and miles across the land. But at my end, in the south, Renn is there. Always ready to greet me with the rising of the sun. *How are you this fine morning?* Tell me a joke, play a game, lift my spirits on a gray, chilly, rainy day. Try to soothe me when I get angry and out of control.

And now.

It's so quiet, so empty, I cannot bear it.

Renn never hurt anybody. People made Renn sick, I'm sure of it. I don't know if I can ever forgive them.

There were times my cousin annoyed me, I admit, when I wasn't in the mood to talk or play or hear a silly pun.

Why did the river watch the news?

I don't know.

To stay current!

But I understand now.

Remember? Renn asked me before the silence. *Remember when we were really loved?*

I didn't answer. But I do. I remember.

Chapter Twenty-Two

ANNALISE

More cancellations. Several cabins sit empty, with clean white sheets on the beds and fresh towels in the bathrooms, but no one to use them. When I open their doors to air them out, they feel forgotten, like a once-favorite toy that's become dusty. Two have a wet-carpet smell. Mom and Dad cancelled all the repairs.

They've been organizing supplies, updating restaurant menus in the binder, and constantly going out to check the lake. Each time one of them comes back, the report is the same: "No change." They put out a few games on the grass in front of the office—a beanbag toss and badminton—but no one's really played them.

The shore is quiet and bare: no blankets, no coolers, no chairs, no people. Just that AVOID CONTACT sign, the sun reflecting off the metal.

My voice hasn't come back either. It's been three days. I tried drinking tea and honey, sucking on lozenges, and even gargling with warm salt water—which was disgusting—but nothing's helped. My throat is still scratchy and raw. Mom told me if it doesn't start getting better soon, I'll need to go to the doctor.

I took a pad of notes from the Thought Wall and have been writing on them when I need to say something. I've been doing a sort of made-up sign language and mouthing words too. Dad said he's enjoying trying to figure out my charades. He sometimes guesses the wrong word on purpose. When I cross my arms and frown, he says, "Just trying to keep it light around here."

After dinner, when I'm signaling to Dad that I'll rinse the dishes, Jess asks if Amy can come over.

"Of course," Mom says. "We're happy to have her."

Jess texts her immediately. Ten minutes later, Jess looks at her phone, then bolts to the door, flings it open, and hugs the girl standing on the porch. "Aims!"

"Jessi-capital *K*-a!"

Amy's as tiny as Jess, and her brown hair goes straight down to the middle of her back. Mom comes out from the kitchen. "Hello," she says. "Nice to finally meet you." Dad's behind Mom. He waves.

Jess points to each of us. "My mom, my dad, my sister Annalise. She's lost her voice."

"Oh, too bad," Amy says.

Jess grabs Amy's hands and they twirl around the

family room together, almost knocking over a lamp. Dad's smiling but Mom says, "Careful!" They fall on the sofa, laughing, holding their stomachs.

"Looks like you two are made for each other," Dad says.

Jess shouts, "Yeah, we're peanut butter and jelly!"

"Ice cream and chocolate syrup!" Amy adds.

"Noodle and doodle!" Jess says. They collapse into giggles again as Jess pulls Amy toward the stairs. "We're going to my room."

"Nice meeting you," Amy calls.

"Have fun," Mom says, turning back toward the kitchen. Dad follows her.

As they walk up the stairs, I hear Amy say, "Any update? Can you go?"

Jess whispers, "No. I've been trying everything to get them to change their minds. I've promised to work at the cabins more and do extra chores at home. But they keep saying they made their decision and it's final."

"Oh, man," Amy says.

They run up. As soon as the door to Jess's room shuts, they start singing and laughing and talking. From the bangs and thuds on the walls and floor, it sounds like they're jumping and dancing too.

Mom brings them a plate of cookies, and I hear Amy sing, "Thank you, Mrs. O! These cookies look delisho!"

They keep it up, even after Dad knocks on the door a few times and tells them to "turn it down a notch."

Later, when I'm in my room, I hear their giggly whispers in the hall, muffled footsteps on the stairs, then the front door opening and closing as Amy leaves. But I don't hear Jess come back up.

I tiptoe down the stairs and peek around the bottom step. Jess is standing in front of the fireplace, quietly staring up at the family picture. Her back is to me. No matter where she goes one day, LA or anywhere else, she'll always have this family tree behind her. These roots.

She turns and spots me before I have a chance to sneak back upstairs.

"What are you doing?" she says softly.

I shrug. "Couldn't sleep," I mouth.

She comes to the stairs and sits on the bottom step. I sit next to her. "I like Amy," I mouth.

"Me too." Jess picks at a thread on the bottom of her shirt. "Annalise, can I tell you something?" She sighs. "I did push Emily."

"You did? Why?"

"Because she said something mean. Something bad."

"What?"

"Before the three-legged race, she came up to me and whispered in my ear, 'Your sister's real mom didn't want her, so she got rid of her.' "

Tears, fast tears. I bite my lip.

"Emily was going in the mud. I didn't even have to think about it."

I sniffle and reach for Jess's hand. She gives mine a squeeze. We stay like that for a minute; then she lets go and stands up. "I didn't tell anyone what Emily said."

"Thank you," I mouth.

She nods and starts to climb the stairs. "I just wanted you to know. G'night."

I stay there on the step in the dark. Jess's door quietly closes.

She complains to Mom and Dad about how they never get mad at me and creates a scene on every found day; then she goes and does this. It makes me think of one of the times I felt like we were there for each other. True sisters.

Jess was eight and I was ten, and we entered the kids' pie-baking contest during the Fourth of July Fest. We combed recipe books, tested at least six different kinds until we decided to design our own—a chocolate pizza pie. Icing for cheese, red gummy circles for tomatoes, Oreo crumbles for sausage. Chocolate pudding for the filling. It was, as Jess kept saying, *spectacular*.

We both thought we'd easily win. There were basic pies—pumpkin, apple—and a few creative ones—a carrot cake pie—but nothing like ours. When we took fifth place, I was pretty upset, but Jess was steaming. A girl in her class, Isabelle, came in first with her pink lemonade pie. She served pink lemonade with it too.

During the awards ceremony, Jess alternated between fuming and crying. I tugged on her sleeve and whispered that we should nab Isabelle's pie. They were all on the judges' table, and no one was there. The crime was, well, easy as pie.

We sidled our way over, ducked, and crawled behind the table. I reached up and took it. We shimmied through the grass by the tent on our stomachs, me with the pie held aloft in one hand; then we got up and ran as fast as we could. We plopped down in back of one of the cabins, laughing and giddy and delirious, and ate the entire thing with our fingers. It was good, maybe a second- or third-placer, but not as good as ours. We agreed that Isabelle only won because her mom was on the planning committee.

After we'd finished stuffing our faces, Jess said, "You're the best sister ever."

And I said, "So are you."

We dug a little hole and buried the evidence—the gooey pie tin. I bet it's still there.

The pie thieves, by the way, were never caught.

* * *

When I get up the next morning, Mom and Dad have already left and Jess's door is shut. I put my ear to the door. No sound. I want to knock, wake her up, ask if she remembers the pie and giggle with her like she did with Amy. But will Jess do that, or will she get upset again about not going to the audition and remind me that Mom and Dad would've said yes if it was me?

I'm not sure. I don't knock.

I get dressed, grab an apple, then head to the cabins. When I'm almost there, I see Vera walking toward Main, her purse over her shoulder.

My throat feels the same. I don't even try talking. I pull a notepad from my pocket and scribble *Are you leaving?*

She nods. "Your parents said they can't pay me right now, not until things get better."

I frown.

She opens her purse and takes out a tissue, then blows her nose. "I was sitting on one of the picnic tables early this morning, thinking about that beautiful old lake, how it's been here longer than you and me and any of us have been alive. My great-gran used to say that water is the mother of the land, nourishing everything. The root of a place, you know? When the water's bad like this, the balance is upset. I'm just sick about it."

I give her a hug and she pats my back. "I hope that bloom goes away real soon," she says.

I'm about to go into the office when I glance hopefully at the lake to see if anything's changed. But it's the same. Green, everywhere. The water bottle is still there, stuck to the surface. I don't care about the sign and the warnings and what the health department people said. I'm getting that bottle off Renn.

I march toward a clump of trees, hunting for a long branch on the ground. I find one, drag it over, and stand at the edge of the water. Stretching as far as I can, I'm able to slowly guide the bottle to the shore. I almost gag when I see clumps of algae clinging to it. I'll have to get something to pick it up with—a paper towel or a plastic bag—and I'm about to get one of those from the office, when I hear something. A sound. So soft, so whispery, it's more like a breath.

Renn?

I quietly lay the branch down and listen.

Another breath? Or did I imagine it?

I scan the algae, thick and slimy everywhere. But then, in the spot where the water bottle had been, I see a tiny opening. Was that there before? I can't remember.

I stand on my tiptoes and lean toward the water. Even if there is a small part where Renn might be able to hear me, I can't say a word.

Chapter Twenty-Three

ANNALISE

My favorite window display was the one Mrs. Alden made for New Year's Day this year. I didn't know how sick she was.

There was a big blue banner across the glass that said HAPPY NEW YEAR! Shiny silver snowflakes turned and glittered, hung from strings. They all had resolutions written on them. Usual ones, like *Start Exercising!* One said *Be a Better Friend!* and another had *Travel to a New City!*

But the one I liked best, in the very center of the window, said *You Can.*

Before the adoption went through, Mrs. Alden took care of me. Mom told me how she bought clothes, knitted blankets, and fed me from a certain kind of bottle because I was fussy. I slept in a cradle they'd used for their sons. She made different-colored bows for my curls, one to match each outfit.

I wish I'd gone inside the store, even just once. I wish I'd said thank you.

I picture her face now as I'm looking out at the lake. It's like she's there with me, the *You Can* snowflake turning slowly above her head.

I step closer to the water, the tips of my shoes inches from the green muck. I open my mouth. "Renn."

My voice comes out raspy and gravelly, and it stings my throat. I peer at the tiny gap. "Renn, can you hear me?"

I wait, crossing my fingers, barely taking a breath. And finally, when I've almost stopped hoping, I hear the quietest sound.

Yes.

I gasp, clap a hand across my heart. "Tell me," I croak, "what I can do to help you?"

Again, a long silence, then four slow words: *The . . . answer . . . is . . . here.*

"I don't understand."

Nothing.

"I don't know what you're trying to tell me."

Nothing.

"Renn?"

The tiny opening is covered up again.

Zach. I've got to find Zach and tell him what I heard.

* * *

I rush toward cabin 8. I haven't seen him since the meeting with the health department a few days ago. What if he and his dad checked out? What if he's gone? He wouldn't leave without telling me, would he?

I reach the cabin and knock on the door several times. Zach's dad answers, and I blow out a relieved breath. His stubble has grown into a beard.

"I'm looking for Zach," I say. My voice is low and hoarse and burns my throat a little, but it's a semi-voice again. "Is he here?"

"No."

"Do you know where he is?"

"He said he was going to the library."

"Okay. If you see him, though, can you give him a message?"

"Sure."

"Tell him that Annalise is looking for him. It's important."

He nods. "All right."

I run to the library and look up and down every aisle and in all the reading rooms, but no Zach. I search everywhere in town. Each tree around the lake where he could be examining something with his magnifying glass. The vacant tent with all the canoes stacked up on the racks. Where could he be? There aren't that many places to hang out in Renn Lake. Maybe he's seeing a movie or he's in one of the stores? Why didn't we ever exchange phone numbers!

Just then, weirdly, my phone buzzes. It's a text from Maya. "EMERGENCY. Tyler's lost his lightsaber."

What I want to respond: *This is not important! The world as we know it is about to end!*

What I do respond: "Oh no. Sad."

"No, this is a major disaster," she replies. "He's going nuts. Won't stop crying. You've got to help me look. We need to find it ASAP. Where are you?"

"I'll meet you at the picnic table by the office in twenty minutes."

When I get there, she's already by the table with the boys. Tyler is red-faced and sobbing uncontrollably. Maya's rubbing his back and talking in a soothing tone. "We'll find it, I promise. Annalise is going to help us. This'll be like that treasure hunt we did, remember?" But Tyler keeps crying. Henry's next to him, holding his lightsaber at his side, pointed down.

"Where have you looked?" I ask.

"Everywhere we've been this morning and yesterday," Maya says.

Henry nods. "Evil forces in the universe took it."

We walk around the lake, Main Street, and the park, with Tyler's bawling quieting into gulps and sniffles. As I'm helping them look, I keep trying to figure out what Renn meant. The answer is *here*?

We don't find the lightsaber. Finally, we return to the picnic table and Maya gives them some pretzels. "I thought I'd gotten this babysitting thing down," she says softly to me.

"You have. It wasn't your fault."

"His mom won't think that." She drops onto the bench.

"Maybe you can offer to buy him another one?"

She waves a hand. "These were limited edition or something. They're not available anymore. I guess I can search online, but who knows if it'll be the exact same kind." She laughs a little. "My aunt would call this *tsuris.*"

"What's that?"

"Serious trouble. She'd be waggling her finger at me too."

"Sorry. Maybe it'll turn up."

"Wait, you got your voice back."

"Yeah."

"One good thing that's happened today, at least. Even though you sound like my grandma. She's smoked since she was fifteen."

"Thanks?"

Zach suddenly strolls out of the office, an open

paperback in his hand. The one place I didn't look! I rush up to him. "I've been trying to find you all morning!"

He tilts his head. "You were? Why?"

"We have to talk. Something happened."

His glasses reflect the sunlight. "What?"

Maya comes over to us. "What's going on, guys?"

"Nothing," I say.

She glances from me to Zach. "Right. I can spot a secret a mile away. Spill."

"It's nothing. Just something with the lake. The algae."

"Tell me. Maybe I can help. You know I'm a natural problem-solver."

I nudge her. "Like finding a lost lightsaber?"

"Okay, except for that."

"Maya!" Tyler shouts. "We forgot to look in the candy shop! When we got the dinosaur eggs!"

"Okay, let's go there now." She grabs the empty pretzel bags. "You know I'm going to get it out of you"—she grins—"eventually." She leaves with the boys, walking backward for a bit to keep an eye on us.

"So what happened?" Zach asks.

"I moved that water bottle with a branch, and there was a little opening in the algae. I heard the lake!"

His eyebrows jump above the top edge of his glasses. "Whoa! What'd you hear?"

" 'The answer is here.' "

“What does that mean?”

“I don’t know. I asked Renn what I could do.”

He nods. “Fascinating.”

I scan the grass, the trees, the sandy dirt, the billions of invisible molecules. “We have to figure this out, Zach. Renn was definitely trying to tell me something. You’ll help, right?”

“Do you even have to ask?”

I grin, then look down at his shoes. “I think you lied to me, and you never learned to tie your shoes.” I kneel and tie the laces. Bunny ears, like I learned when I was little, and double knots. I stand up when I finish, and he has this crooked smile on his face.

“Why’d you do that? I told you, they’ll just untie again.”

“And I told you, not if you do double knots.”

He takes off his glasses, blinks several times.

I gently knock his shoulder with my fist. “Come on. We have a puzzle to solve.”

Chapter Twenty-Four

ANNALISE

Zach and I huddle on the sofa in the office for the next hour with our phones, reading everything we can find online about algal blooms in lakes.

I read more about the treatments they mentioned at the meeting. They're supposed to kill algae, or at least stop it from growing. But they all sound complicated, and sometimes more harmful than the algae itself. And anyway, none of them give me a clue about how the answer can be *here.* Renn's words are a mystery.

I look up and notice Mom standing in front of us. I rub my eyes. "Hi."

She smiles. "Oh, thank goodness. I thought you were in a coma and I'd have to call nine-one-one."

"Ha. But actually, sort of."

"Dad and I have been tackling some projects we usually don't have time for. When you're ready to take a break from whatever you two have been so intent on, would you mind bringing the items in the lost-and-found bin over to Castaway? It's time we got rid of it all."

"Sure."

"Actually, a break sounds good." Zach clicks off his phone. "Mind if I come?"

"Okay." I go over to the front desk and pull out the bin.

Mom gets a big laundry bag from the supply closet. "Tell Toni I'll get the bag later."

"I will." Zach and I start piling armfuls of clothes, shoes, hats, towels, and other junk into the bag. We need a second bag, there's so much stuff. Zach picks up one and I grab the other. We maneuver them out the door. I glance back at Mom, hunched over her keyboard. Her fingers aren't moving.

I put my bag down. "I'll be back in one sec."

Mom looks up and dabs the corner of her eye with a tissue as I come into the office. "I think you got everything," she says.

"Mom . . . I ran into Vera earlier. She told me."

"It's just temporary. We'll rehire her, as soon as things are better."

I unhook the clasp of my necklace and lay it gently on the counter. "I want you to return this. You can use the money for whatever you need to pay for."

She stares at the necklace for a moment, then pushes it toward me. "Oh, Annalise. That's so generous. Thank you for offering, but please keep it."

I don't pick it up. "But I heard you and Dad talking about that time with the tornado."

She comes around and hugs me. "There've always been challenges, and this is certainly one of them, but we'll think of something. Dad and I have been discussing ideas. If Gramps taught me anything, it was to rise up against the odds." She takes the necklace and puts it back on me.

I hesitate. "You're sure?"

She nods. "Go ahead, Zach's waiting."

I walk out and grab the bag again.

"Everything okay?" Zach asks.

"Sort of." Mom seemed positive, but the shore is still empty. "C'mon," I say. We start walking toward town.

He sighs. "While you were talking to your mom, I was going over everything I read but nothing's jumping out."

"I feel like we're never going to find out what Renn was trying to tell me."

Zach's carrying his bag against his chest. "*The answer is here, the answer is here.* You're sure that's what you heard?"

"Definitely. Maybe we shouldn't think about it for a while?"

"Yeah. Good idea. Give our brains a rest."

We cross the street. It's quiet on Main. "So it looks like you're done with the contacts?" I ask.

"I think so."

"Why *did* you want them?"

He stops and plunks his bag on the ground. "I wanted to be a different person." He half-smiles. "I had a whole plan, made a long list. The contacts were the first thing. The new me! I was going to lift weights, grow out my hair, learn French. I'd be really cool. Stupid stuff."

I set my bag down too and glance at his arms, still skinny and bony. "How come you wanted to be a different person?"

"Because then Leo . . ." His voice trails off.

"Oh."

He looks at the sidewalk. "Then he'd see me differently. Want me back."

I nod.

"After the breakup, I felt invisible, and like I couldn't get enough oxygen. Nothing was like it used to be. I know how Renn feels." He picks up the bag and hoists it over his shoulder, then strides ahead. He reaches Castaway, jerks open the door, and wrestles the bag inside.

I take my bag and follow him.

Toni, the owner, is perched on a stool behind the counter, eating a salad. "Bringing me some presents?"

We drop the bags on the floor. "Yeah," I say. "From the lost-and-found bin."

"Wonderful!" Toni wiggles off the stool and comes over. Her long, beaded earrings swing back and forth as she digs through the bags. "Most of this is in decent shape. Do your parents need a receipt for the donation?"

"Yeah, thanks."

She goes to the counter and I steal a glance at Zach, but he's looking away. I can tell he doesn't want to talk anymore.

The shelves and racks are filled with clothes and shoes. I always wonder who owned this stuff before. The fuzzy white sweater with the red satin bows, maybe a popular city girl? The black boots with chains and scuffed heels, a motorcycle dude? How and why do they end up here, waiting for someone to wear them again? To love them.

Toni hands me the receipt. "Would you two do me a favor and carry these to the back room? My knees have been giving me some trouble lately."

"Okay. And my mom said she'd get the bags later."

Toni nods. "Sure."

When I drag a bag into the small room, it falls over and a few things spill out. And there, peeking out of a rolled-up towel, is the tip of a lightsaber. I pull it out. "At least this mystery is solved! Tyler lost it and we looked everywhere." I text Maya.

Zach says, "Lost things are always where you never think to look."

"Definitely."

As Zach and I are heading back to the cabins, Maya, Henry, and Tyler sprint toward us. Tyler's little arms are outstretched and his legs are whirling so fast, I'm sure he's going to trip and land face-first on the sidewalk. But he doesn't. I hand it over, and he points the lightsaber toward the sky and spins around. "I'm back! Watch out, evil forces!"

Maya hugs me. "The lost-and-found bin! Thank you so much! I should've thought of that!"

The boys run ahead, poking flowerpots and light posts, slashing benches and trash cans.

"I owe you big-time," Maya says. "Thankfully you found it before someone bought it."

"You don't owe me. It was just lucky."

Henry slaps a row of bushes and a bunch of leaves fall to the ground.

"Don't hurt the bushes! They're alive!" Maya calls, then says, "I have to tell Mrs. Olsen. She'll be so happy. Who knew it was right under my nose all along." Maya pulls out her phone.

Zach and I glance at each other. I feel like we both know the answer is right under our noses too. We just need to stumble on it, like the lightsaber.

Chapter Twenty-Five

TRU

I heard it too. What Renn said to the girl.

At my far northern end, there is another body of water, a small, quiet lake that people named Violet, with a delicate, lacy shoreline and a purply color in the moonlight. Once, Violet was very sick too. Almost died. But the people who lived nearby discovered a way. They cared for Violet. They saved that little lake. And for that, I am grateful.

I must show them, the girl and the boy. I must get them to understand what they need to do.

I course my waters toward Renn, to the reeds that grow in the cove, and use my force to pull them out by their roots.

It is time for me to open my heart and trust again.

It is time for me to make things right.

Chapter Twenty-Six

ANNALISE

The next morning, two more reservations are cancelled, and the people in cabin 3 check out early. Mom and Dad sit on the sofa, shuffling through bills, deciding which ones to pay and which ones to put off. They've put me in charge of the front desk, but the office is a ghost town.

Dad says, "Jackie, we have to do something, and fast. Let's go through that list of ideas again."

Mom moves her pen down a pad of paper. "We talked about some type of sporting event, an art fair, a concert, a dog show. We might be able to get people here, but these are all going to take a lot of planning." She glances out the window toward Renn. "And a lot of time."

"Agree, but what choice do we have at this point?" Dad sits back against the cushions. "What about getting some groups here for meetings? Like clubs and organizations."

Mom nods. "I'll make some calls, get the word out. Maybe someone needs a last-minute place."

"Okay," Dad says. "And I'll send out emails to everyone at the chamber of commerce."

Jess barges in, Amy behind her. "This is the office," Jess says. "And that's the Thought Wall. You can add a note if you want."

"So fun!" Amy peels off a yellow square. She scribbles on it, then sticks it to the wall. *Wish Me Luck,* with a star around the words.

"Oh, for sure!" Jess cries, and hugs her. "Good luck!" She looks at us. "The audition's tomorrow. Aims is *so* going to get picked. I just know it."

They chatter about the audition—how many people might be there, who'll be conducting it, when she'll find out if she made it. Amy keeps calling Jess "Jessi-capital *K*-a." And my sister has said, "You are *so* right," about ten times, laughing. But it's not her laugh.

Amy cups her hand, whispers in Jess's ear. I'm close enough to hear. "You're sure you can't go?"

Jess rolls her eyes. "No means no."

Does my sister even get what's going on? I ask Mom if I can take a break. She nods and picks up her phone. I walk down to the lake, shade my eyes with one hand and look out, hoping for something promising, but it's as sickly green as ever.

I spot Zach at the far end of the shore, crouching down. I head toward him. He's examining something with his magnifying glass. His hair isn't in the usual ponytail; it's loose and wavy, just touching his shoulders.

"Hey," I say. "What's up?"

"Hi. I was just going to look for you. I found something that strikes me as very odd."

A bunch of the long, thin reeds have been pulled out by their roots and are lying flat and limp on the ground. "That's weird."

"Yes, it is. There wasn't a storm last night, and I don't think this was from an animal—no tracks." He peers at the roots through the glass. "What, or who, yanked these out so violently?"

I kneel, examine the roots too. "How do you know it was violent?"

"It just seems as if they were ripped out by something. The fibers are split, like they were torn apart. Pieces of the roots are everywhere."

"Maybe the algal bloom caused this."

He tucks the glass into his pocket. "That's not what they do. They just zap all the oxygen and nutrients from the water. And besides, roots are pretty strong. They're like anchors. Some tree roots go as deep as the height of the tree."

"Vera told me something about roots. . . . Oh, that water is the root of a place."

He moves one of the reeds with the toe of his shoe. "I wonder if these guys talk to each other too, the way scientists think trees do."

There's so much on this planet that I know nothing about. That maybe none of us will ever know. It hurts my head to think about that. Below the dirt, in the air, in the depths of water. Millions of living, breathing, hidden worlds.

Vera said when the water's bad, the balance is upset, and the people at the meeting said it too. Like the whole world is resting on a giant scale, and the littlest thing can tip it over.

I get up and scan the water for any sort of opening, but there isn't one. Just some of the torn-off reeds, stuck in the algae.

"Zach?"

He stands too. "Yeah?"

"What you said yesterday about being invisible? I saw you in the field at my school, reading. And when you were examining a tree with your magnifying glass, before we knew each other. You're not invisible."

He looks out at the water. "I don't feel like that here. It's so different from my apartment building where people barely say hi to each other, and my school, where everyone has to be the best." He laughs. "Renn Lake is calming. Like you're wrapped in a giant fleece blanket that's around the whole town."

I touch his arm. "Exactly how I feel."

He covers my fingers for a second with his hand. "Do you ever think about where you came from?"

"Sometimes."

"You could do a post on social media, look for your birth mom. People do that."

"I don't want to."

"Yeah, I get that. I'm not sure I would either." He looks at the scattered reeds. "I guess we'll never know what pulled these out of the ground."

I study the roots—their strong network of thin, intertwined fibers. Roots are underneath everything, keeping it all anchored. The reeds. The trees, the lake, the cabins. Mom and her dad and grandpa. The arrowhead and the old key that washed up. The mysteriously named Sage Street, the pile of forgotten things in the lost-and-found bin, even the coins people leave in the cabins. All of it . . . it's the roots of Renn Lake.

I trace the necklace with the tip of my finger. "Roots are here, even if you can't see them."

He smiles.

"Here." *Here.* I gasp. "Zach!"

He jumps. "What?"

"It's not chemicals, or a machine that blows air into the water." I circle my arms. "The answer is here! Something right around us. Dirt and lost arrowheads and buried keys and leaves and *roots*!"

Zach stares at me, then shouts, "Wait! I'm so spacy sometimes! It was such a small part of the science unit, I didn't even think of it. But my teacher said there are some plants that eat up bad algae."

"What!" A shock runs through me. "You're just remembering that *now*!"

"I didn't make the connection. There was a lot of information in that class. I filled up four entire notebooks!"

"This has to be what Renn was trying to tell me."

Zach's already tapping his phone. "Right, right! Floating plant islands," he says. "Their roots dangle into the water and basically soak up the excess nutrients and algae. It's genius, really. This website says they were used on a contaminated lake in Montana. And Illinois. And other places too—China, New Zealand, Canada. It took time—months, or close to a year in some cases—but it worked. The plant islands mimicked wetlands." He looks up. "Of course! Wetlands are natural water purifiers. They strain out the bacteria."

I want to do a hundred cartwheels across the shore. "Let's go tell my dad! C'mon! We found a solution!" And it *was* right under our noses.

I start to run, but he doesn't move. "What are you waiting for?" I yell over my shoulder.

Zach slides his phone into his pocket, then sprints to catch up with me, his hair blowing behind him. "Not to be negative, but don't you think those people from the health department would know about this?"

I stop, cross my arms. "Well, if they do, I'm going to remind them. *They* can't hear Renn. I can."

Chapter Twenty-Seven

ANNALISE

Maya's sitting at the picnic table outside the office. I rush past, shouting, "Hi! Bye!"

"Wait, what's going on?" she calls. "I just texted you. Wanna come with me to get a manicure? I'm free! Mrs. Olsen took the boys to the doctor. I could really use some pampering."

"No, sorry, can't right now!"

"What's the matter?"

"Nothing! We may have solved the puzzle!"

She looks from Zach to me. "What puzzle? Is this your secret?"

I bang open the door. "I think we found a way to get rid of the algae!"

Zach and I run inside and Maya follows. Dad's behind the front desk on the phone. I wave my arms, then whisper, "We need to tell you something!"

Dad raises his eyebrows, shakes his head. Then keeps *talking*!

I grab a sticky note and write *IMPORTANT!* but he still doesn't hang up! I can't help it, I sort of morph into my sister—pacing back and forth in front of the desk, doing a couple of stomps and several huffs—until he finally ends the call.

"Okay, what's the emergency?"

"Dad!" I shout. "Sorry to barge in, but Zach and I found a solution!"

"Well, maybe," Zach says.

"No, not *maybe,* yes!" I add one last stomp. "Listen. There was a contaminated lake in Montana. They made these islands with plants on them, and the roots dangled into the water and ate up the bad algae! The lake got better, just from the plants!" I snap my fingers. "Problem solved!"

"That's amazing!" Maya says.

"They work like a wetland," Zach explains, reading from his phone. "The plant roots grow through a porous soil base and absorb the nitrogen and phosphorus—"

"You can show him all that later," I interrupt. "Dad, you have to call the people from the health department. The bloom isn't going away. We have to do this! Now!"

"Hold on." Dad puts up a hand. "I'm sure they're aware of these plant islands, wouldn't you think?"

"They didn't mention it at the meeting!"

"Annalise, we have to be patient. They said the best thing is to let the bloom dissipate on its own. They're in charge."

"It's been days! Nothing's changed!"

"Remember, they said it can take weeks, even months. The other lake might have had different conditions," Dad says softly. "You don't know what was going on there, or if it was the same as here. The shape of the lake, the depth, the type of algae—all that makes a difference."

I look at Sophie's note with the frowny face: *The lake is sad.* "Dad, why can't we just call? Ask if they know about the plant islands?"

Mom comes into the office, glances around at us. "What's going on?"

Dad grabs his phone. "Okay, I'll call."

"They figured out how to get rid of the algae," Maya tells Mom.

"Really? How?" Mom asks.

Zach explains the floating plant islands. "Very interesting," she says. "What kinds of plants do they use?"

"Anything that likes water." Zach shows her pictures on his phone. "Iris, sedges, cattail, some types of ferns."

Dad starts talking to someone and we listen. He mentions the islands, then stops midsentence. Long pause.

"Yes," he finally says. "Right. Of course. I understand." He hangs up. The entire call was about two minutes.

"They know about the islands," he says.

"Great!" I shout. "Are they going to use them?"

"It's what I thought. They don't have the budget or resources. They're sticking with the current plan for all blooms. It should eventually go away on its own, depending on the weather."

"So?"

He puts a hand on my shoulder. "So we just have to wait. It's out of our control."

"But it's *not* out of our control!" I yell. "We can *do* something! And we *have* to! It's our responsibility to take care of the lake."

"Annalise," Dad says. "Listen to me—"

"No! Why won't they try the islands? Or do anything? It's dying! We have to get the algae off so the lake can breathe!"

So Renn can talk to me. And listen.

Dad moves toward me, arms outstretched. "Don't worry. It'll be all right. I promise."

Mom's right behind him. "Gramps used to say—"

"No!" I back away. "You don't know that it'll be all right! Some things are *never* going to be completely all right. What happened to me will always be there, no matter what you say or do."

Mom's fingers flutter to her heart. Dad covers his mouth with a hand. Their faces. I've stung them. I threw those words like darts, when they had nothing to do with it. And the words can't ever be erased.

Zach and Maya are standing by the Thought Wall, surrounded by yellow squares. People's wishes and hopes and feelings.

"But I can help Renn," I blurt, and run out.

I weave around towering pine trees, their low branches scratching my arms. I stumble on the dirt path until I get to the last cabin. It's empty.

I fall onto the front step, my face hot and sweaty, curling into a ball and wrapping my arms around my legs.

I hear heavy footsteps and look up. Zach and Maya are running toward me.

When they get to the cabin, Zach's wheezing a little. "You going out for cross-country or something?"

"Ha," I croak.

"Are you okay?" Maya asks. "That was some big stuff back there."

I sniffle. "If they're not going to do anything, I have to."

Zach shakes his head. "You heard what your dad said. They're in charge. We need to be patient."

"Forget patience. I'm done waiting. I'm going to make the plant islands and put them in the lake."

"*What?*" Zach says. "Annalise, you can't just—"

"I can." I picture the silver snowflake in Mrs. Alden's window. "And I only have one question. Are you with me?"

Neither of them says anything. Are they thinking this is the worst idea they've ever heard, or the best?

I uncurl and stand up, brush off my shorts. "I guess it doesn't matter if you are or aren't, because I'm doing it anyway." My voice catches. "I am *not* abandoning Renn."

Maya looks at me, then raises an eyebrow. "Interesting thing about Wisconsin. I've heard my parents talk about how it's a home rule state."

"What does that mean?"

"It means that towns can make their own decisions about things that affect them."

"Hmm," Zach says.

Maya smiles. "Exactly."

"So . . ." I look from one to the other.

"So I'm in if you're in," Maya says.

Zach throws up his hands. "I'm outvoted. Where do we start?"

I let out a breath. "With our own plan. We're going to save the lake."

Chapter Twenty-Eight

ANNALISE

"Let's meet first thing in the morning and figure everything out," I say. "How to make the plant islands, what supplies we need, and, mostly, how to get them in the lake without anyone seeing. Or trying to stop us."

Maya pulls out her phone and groans. "I gotta get the boys. Mrs. Olsen needs to go back to work."

"But you'll help tomorrow?" I ask.

"I promised the boys I'd take them to a movie. They'll be so mad if I don't. I'll find you as soon as it's over." She hurries off.

Zach says he has some money left over from his birthday, and I tell him about my coin jar. "I have seventeen dollars and one cent."

"And I have about twenty bucks. I don't know for sure, but that should be enough." He pushes up his glasses. "You're absolutely positive you want to do this? We could get in huge trouble."

"Not a doubt in my mind. Renn *told* me."

"Great." He rolls his eyes. "We can explain that to the cops when they arrest us."

"Ha. Are you nervous?"

He laughs. "All the time. It's kinda like my permanent status."

"You can back out any time, you know."

"I'm not backing out."

"Good. Don't tell anyone, by the way."

He nods. "I won't."

"See you tomorrow, then. Nine o'clock, by the reeds."

We finally exchange phone numbers and say goodbye. I can't face Mom and Dad yet, not after what I said, so I walk home and spend the rest of the day reading everything I can find online about plant islands.

They don't sound too hard to make. There's a base with holes in it for the roots, and the top has soil and plants. The islands can be large or small. In pictures, they look like miniature floating gardens.

I'm reading one last website when a text from Maya pops up on my phone: "U home?"

"Yeah."

"Meet me out back?"

"Okay."

There's no fence between our backyards, just a long rectangle of grass stretching from my house to hers, and

Maya's old swing set in the middle. When I come outside, she's sitting on one of the swings, hands folded in her lap. I sit in the other one.

"You look kind of lost and lonely without Henry and Tyler next to you," I say.

"Now that you mention it."

"You're lost and lonely?"

She digs her heels into the dirt patch below the swing. "I'm happy that you and Zach found something that might clean up the algae . . . but okay, I'm just going to say it. Do you and him have a thing?"

"A thing? Me and Zach?"

"Yeah. You've been spending practically every moment with him. We've hardly hung out."

"Because you're babysitting all day and then you're wiped out at night."

Her shoulders sag. "I always knew when one of us got a boyfriend, it'd change stuff . . ."

"Maya, Zach's not my boyfriend. He's gay. We're friends."

She covers her eyes with a hand. "Oh. Well, now I feel like a complete idiot."

I shrug. "It's okay. I would've thought the same thing, I guess."

"Sorry. My bad." She sighs. "This is what else I've been thinking: I'm never having kids."

"Really?"

"At least, not twin boys." She walks the swing back, then lifts her feet and lets go. I start pumping too. The metal frame squeaks and wobbles from our weight.

"Are we too big for the swings?" she shouts, getting higher and higher. "Because it should be a rule that you never outgrow your childhood swing set!"

"Agree!"

First, we're going the same; then she pumps faster and we're swinging opposite. Maya's hair loosens from her bun and blows wildly around her face. My hands get sweaty gripping the chains. For a few minutes, we're eight again, swinging after school, kicking off our shoes in the air, laughing about the blimperfly and teasing each other and singing songs from the third-grade concert. "This Land Is Your Land" . . . "Down by the Riverside" . . . "Lean on Me" . . . I can hear them all in my head until the creaking of the pole gets louder and more threatening. I slow down, and Maya does too.

She reaches her hand out between the swings and I grab it. We hold on to each other, arms connected across the dirt. We don't have to say anything.

Her dad calls from the back of her house. "Maya? Oh, hi, Annalise." I wave. "Maya?" he repeats. "The disaster that is your room?"

She gives me a squeeze and lets go. "I told the dentists

I'd clean it." She rolls her eyes and gets up. "They also want me to donate part of my babysitting money to charity. Tzedakah. Doing what's right. But I haven't said yes to that."

"We're counting on you to help with the fest, Annalise," her dad says. "Lots of work to do."

"Can we still have it?" I ask.

"It's on the shore, not in the water. We're going to have it, algae or no algae."

Maya walks backward toward her house. She crosses her eyes and sticks out her tongue.

I laugh. "See you tomorrow."

"As soon as the movie's over." She does a double thumbs-up and goes inside.

Later, when Mom and Dad get home and we all sit down for dinner, it feels awkward. Everyone's quiet, even Jess. Her elbow is on the table and her face is propped up in her hand. She's staring off into space. The clinking of forks and glasses echoes through the kitchen, as loud as if they're being dropped, and we're all avoiding each other's eyes.

After we finish eating, Mom clears the table, then starts rinsing dishes. Dad goes out to the porch and sits in the swing. The skin on Mom's hands is shiny and glistening, and I can see the back of Dad's head through the window, his loose-thread, wispy hair brushing the edge of his shirt collar.

The words I spat out earlier are whirling around me like windswept leaves. I don't know how to get them to settle. I don't know what to say to make it better.

That night, I hardly sleep. My heart's too sore and my head's too full.

I wake up late the next morning, cotton-mouthed and disoriented. I sit up in bed, try to shake off the fuzziness, then remember I'm supposed to meet Zach. I text him and say I'm going to be late but I'll get there as soon as I can. Brush teeth, get dressed, grab a granola bar. No one's around; the house is sun-warm and quiet.

I need to bring my coins to buy the supplies for the plant islands. I reach behind the boots in my closet for the jar, and . . . nothing. I feel around, pick up the boots and some shoes, and shove aside my backpack and a basket of books. It's not there.

I stand up, confused and starting to panic. Did I put it somewhere else, and don't remember? Did Mom clean my closet and move it? I search the rest of my room, and when I get to my dresser, there's a piece of paper in the exact spot where I used to keep the coins.

Dear Annalise,

I borrowed your money. I'll pay you back, every cent, I swear. I needed it for the audition fee. I went with Amy and her mom. By the time you read this, I'll have a part in the movie. Please don't tell Mom and Dad. I have to do this. It's in me as much as the cabins are in you.

Love,
JessiKa
Your soon-to-be-famous sister

I'm frozen next to my dresser, the note in my shaking hands. She took my coins! She didn't borrow them, she didn't ask, she just snuck into my room and helped herself. How will I be able to buy the supplies now?

That day she asked me how much I had, did she have this in mind all along? And, she actually went to the audition, after Mom and Dad said no a hundred times! And I'm not supposed to tell them?

I slam my closet door, then storm into Jess's room. Heaps of clothes and spilled makeup are all over the floor. I tear out of the house, texting Zach to tell him that something happened and I don't know when I can meet him. Twenty minutes later, I burst into the office. Mom and Dad both jump.

"Hi. One, I'm sorry. Really, really sorry. I don't even know where to start or what to say."

Mom gets teary immediately. "We understand, honey. Or at least we try to, but I know we'll never be able to completely—"

I wave a hand. "Two, Jess is gone."

"What?" Dad says. "What do you mean, *gone*?"

I hand him the note. Mom reads over his shoulder. "No," he says. "She didn't."

Mom's mouth is hanging open. "I can't believe it. She wasn't in the house, you're sure?"

"She wasn't there."

Mom grabs her phone and scrolls through the contacts. "I don't even have Amy's mom's phone number. I should've gotten it." She calls Jess and we listen to the rings.

Dad pulls his keys from his pocket. "I'm driving to Madison. Right now."

"Wait, let me try to get Amy's mom's number. I'll call some mothers of the girls in Jess's class," Mom says.

"No, I'm going. It's just an hour away. She can't pull something like this."

"We don't even know where the audition's taking place. You could drive all over the city. What was it, Celery Productions? I can't remember!"

"Cucumber." I'm already searching on my phone for

a movie being filmed in Madison. "Here." I show Dad my screen. "This has to be it."

He grabs a sticky note, writes down the information. "It's an alien sci-fi movie! That's what she wants to audition for?"

"Go!" Mom shouts. "I'll keep calling her."

"I'll find her," Dad says, and rushes out the door. Mom and I look at each other. I hug her, say it'll be all right. My arms feel strong around her.

"If anything happens to Jess . . . ," Mom says.

"Jessi-*kuh*? That girl is made of steel."

Mom cry-laughs, then steps back. "Annalise, I honestly didn't know you were feeling all that. I can't imagine what must go through your mind sometimes. We never wanted you to think it was your fault. That person's choice wasn't about you."

"I know."

She blows her nose with a tissue. "It's terrible that you were abandoned. There's no getting around that. But it happened."

I nod.

"Now you get to decide what happens next."

We don't say anything else, but it feels like my dart-thrown words aren't as sharp. And the whirling leaves are slowing down.

The door to the office bangs open and Zach comes in. "What's going on?"

Long sigh. "My sister went to Madison this morning."

He frowns. "Wait. By herself?"

"No." I turn to Mom. "I have to talk to Zach a sec, okay? I'll be right back."

"Go ahead."

I tip my head toward the door and Zach and I go outside. "My sister wanted to go to a movie audition in Madison, but my parents said she couldn't, so she went with her friend without telling them. My dad just left to go find her."

"Whoa. How old is she?"

"Ten."

"That's pretty daring."

"Yeah, that's my sister. She wants to be a famous actress and get out of Renn Lake as soon as she can. Anyway, she took all my coins. My money's gone."

"That puts a little dent in our plan."

"Right. Unless your twenty bucks will be enough to cover everything we need. Although I don't want you to pay for all this. You don't even live here. It isn't your lake."

"I don't mind."

"I can ask Maya to help."

"Okay. But, actually, I was wondering, where are we

going to get the supplies? Because if we're keeping this a secret, we can't ask one of our parents for a ride. After—don't faint or anything—after going out to dinner with me last night, my dad thinks he had a breakthrough and he's back at it. So it has to be somewhere we can walk to, right? Maybe, like, a garden center?"

I knew this was coming.

Zach asks, "Is there a place that's close by?"

"Yes." I slowly raise my arm and point to Alden's.

Chapter Twenty-Nine

TRU

I wasn't sure the reeds would work. The girl and the boy are smart; they figured it out. But now they are stuck. Like Renn.

Deep down in my depths, I know this is my fault. I knew that what I did would one day come back to haunt me.

I was so angry that night. Watching those wild young men throwing things as if I were a garbage dump. First, the slick rubber tires. Two of them, rolled down my bank. Then the cans of paint, one after the other, poured into me. Torrents of red and black and orange, thick and pungent and stinging. And then the pocketknife, slipping from one of their hands and slicing through my waters.

They were laughing. Punching each other. Drinking from bottles, which ended up in me too. It was a game.

After they were finished, they left in their car, wheels digging into the dirt, fumes lingering.

I erupted. I struck anything and everything in my path. My current was out of control.

In the distance, I heard Renn's voice, but I was too worked up to listen. I wanted revenge.

I didn't see the canoe at first.

She was suddenly there, paddling along. I didn't know. I didn't know what had happened.

I didn't know about the baby.

Chapter Thirty

ANNALISE

"Zach," I say. "There's something I need to do. Something I should have done a long time ago."

He nods, seems to understand.

"I'll text you later and we'll figure something out."

"Okay." He turns, meanders toward his cabin, stopping to put his ear to a tree trunk. His shoelaces have double knots.

I walk back into the office. Mom's in the same spot, holding her phone and staring at the screen.

"Any news from Dad?" I ask. "Or Jess?"

She shakes her head. "Not yet. And she's still not answering. I'm going back and forth between being angry and worried that something's going to happen to her."

"But she's with Amy and her mom, right?"

"Unless she gets it in her head to go off on her own. Introduce herself to a casting director. You know your sister."

I do.

Mom glances at me. "Everything okay?"

"Sort of . . . I have to go somewhere. I don't want to say where, but I promise, I'm not leaving town."

"It's somewhere in Renn Lake?"

"Yes."

A long pause. She studies my face. "Text me when you get there."

"I will. It's not far." I slide off the Renn Lake Rentals cap and put it on the counter, then go out.

No cap pulled down to my eyes, no hat that I pretended was armor. One foot after the other. One thousand, eight hundred and seventeen steps. In my head, pounding on repeat: *You have to do this. For Renn.*

Standing in front of Alden's Gift Emporium: Flora, Fauna, and Whatnot, I almost smile at the pink flamingo floaties still in the window. The flamingo closest to me has one eye that's a black dot and the other that's a dash. Like it's winking.

I text Mom, then wrap my fingers around the brass door handle. I turn it, almost surprised that I can, and take the one thousandth, eight hundredth and eighteenth step.

Inside.

No one is there, not even Mr. Alden. The room is filled

with leafy plants and flowers in pots and baskets. A worn, scratched wood floor. A red wagon holding a giant teddy bear, its paw resting on the handle. Glossy gazing balls are on metal stands. A wicker chair, a lacy pillow, and a metal bucket with pretend ice cubes line the far wall.

"Can I help you with something?"

Gray hair, eyes a darker gray. Crisscrossed wrinkles on his cheeks. Loose, pleated pants and a blue collared shirt, tucked in neatly.

"Oh," Mr. Alden says. "Hello."

I swallow. "Hi."

I don't know what to say. I don't know how to decide what happens next. I feel weightless, but like I'm falling, sinking, drowning. I'm aching to run but I can't anymore.

"I'm glad you're here, Annalise."

I try not to cry. I try to hear Renn telling me it's just wood, brick, glass, and it can't hurt me.

Mr. Alden and I stand opposite each other for a few seconds, bits of dust floating in and out of strips of sunlight. Then I blurt, "I'm sorry I didn't come to the funeral."

He touches the gold band on his finger. "I'm not much for funerals myself, to tell the truth. They're mighty depressing. And the person who's gone doesn't know who's there or not."

"Still, though. I should've come."

"Thank you. It's very kind of you to say."

I wait for the shadow carrying baby me in its arms to appear, slither down my throat and shatter my heart.

But there's only the slow-turning dust, orbiting in its own starry galaxy. Instead of the shadow putting me down, what I feel is Mrs. Alden's strong hands picking me up and soothing me.

"Can I see it?" My words are barely a whisper. "Where I was."

He nods. "Of course. I knew one day you'd want to." He motions, and I follow him through the store.

In the back, a weathered wood door is partly open. He steps outside, into a garden that curves around the side. More plants and flowers. A bench, a trellis, and flat, sand-colored stones are scattered on the ground. Words are carved on them. DREAM. BELIEVE. CHOOSE JOY. And LOVE GROWS HERE.

"Where was it?" I ask softly.

He walks to the doorway and stands just inside. "Right here. We used to carry baby things. Blankets and bibs and such. The bassinet was beautiful. Handmade. One of a kind."

"What happened to it?"

"After the investigation, it didn't seem right to keep it in the store. I offered it to a family over in Jonesville.

They didn't have much money, and they were expecting. I'm sorry it's not here for you to see."

"It's very peaceful back here. Kind of . . . hidden away."

"Yes. Sometimes I like to come out here and think. Clear my head."

"Mr. Alden . . . can you tell me about that night? I think I'm ready to know."

He goes to the bench and sits down, pats the seat beside him. I sit too. His chest rises, then falls with a long breath.

"It had been so busy that day. A busload of seniors from Milwaukee, several school field trips. Full up at your parents' cabins. People in every corner of Renn Lake.

"It was late. We had just closed and locked up. Viv was sweeping the floor, and I was at the cash register, getting everything back in order. Suddenly, a surge of water flooded this whole area, right where we're sitting. It came out of nowhere. There wasn't a storm. It wasn't raining. I rushed back here, and then I saw Viv holding you."

I know the story. But still, not from him. "What did you think, when you saw me?"

He gazes toward the doorway and his eyes get watery. "I thought that someone must have been in a terribly hopeless situation to leave a baby. People can do unthinkable things when they're desperate."

Through the bushes in the garden, I can glimpse a bit of the lake beyond the sidewalk. "Mr. Alden . . . ," I start, and then stop. Do I really want to ask this? Do I want to know the answer?

"Yes?"

I look toward the doorway. I have to ask, even if I'm not sure I want to know. "Do you, or did Mrs. Alden, remember seeing anyone in the store that day with . . . me?"

He nods, like he knew what I was going to say. "The police questioned us about that, of course. But, regrettably, no. We must've gone over that day a thousand times, but we never could recall seeing anyone with a newborn baby. I'm sorry."

"I guess I'll never know exactly what happened."

"I suppose you won't." He folds his hands in his lap. "I've always thought that when we can't find the answer to something, as much as we might want to, it's best to accept that not knowing might be the answer."

"That's hard."

"It is."

We're silent for a few minutes. Leaves and flower petals flutter in the warm breeze. The words bubble up in me then, burn on my tongue and become so bitter I have to let them out.

"I guess . . . I wasn't wanted." I've never said that to anyone. But maybe I've always thought it.

"I wouldn't look at it that way," he says. "You may not know where you came from and why you ended up here, but believe me, you were wanted."

A squirrel hops through the garden, an acorn in its mouth. I had so many other questions tumbling around in my head while I was walking over. But they don't seem to matter anymore. A stripe of sunlight falls across the LOVE GROWS HERE stone. Maybe the person who left me had a reason.

"I'll tell you something else," Mr. Alden says. "Those few months my wife and I took care of you before you went to the Olivers were wonderful. Our boys had already grown up and were off on their own. Despite what happened, you were a delightful baby. I know newborns can't smile—at least, that's what I was always told—but you did. I'm sure of it."

A tear plops onto my hand.

He offers me a handkerchief from his shirt pocket. It's white, folded in a small square, and has a blue embroidered flower. "This was Viv's. I like to keep a part of her next to me."

I dry my eyes, then hand it back to him.

"Why don't you hold on to it? I have more at home."

The handkerchief is delicate and soft. I trace the stitching with my fingertips. I need to say what I never said to Mrs. Alden. At least I can tell him.

"Thank you. For finding me. For taking care of me."

He pats my hand. "We loved you like you were our own. Viv wanted to keep you, raise you herself. But we were too old. She knew that." He shakes his head. "Holding a tiny baby . . . makes you feel like you can start all over again."

I sniffle. "I wish I'd known her. I wish I'd come in before—"

"It's all right. She knew you."

A yellow petal drifts to the ground.

"She had a name for you, you know. We weren't going to call you the 'Alden's Baby.'" He looks off. "We adored our sons, but Viv longed for a daughter. If we'd had one, we would've named her Margaret. So that's what we called you."

Lots of tears now. The handkerchief smells like soap, and lemon.

He picks up a brittle leaf from the ground and crumbles it between his fingers, then lets the breeze take the pieces. "Ah, well. Anything else you'd like to know?"

Only one question left.

"Mr. Alden, have you ever heard of floating plant islands?"

Chapter Thirty-One

ANNALISE

The more I explain how plant islands work, the more I feel like roots are growing right out of my toes and anchoring me; keeping me upright, like those flamingos in the window.

"Have you mentioned this idea to the people from the health department?" Mr. Alden asks.

"My dad called."

"And?"

I tell him what they said. He rubs the side of his jaw as I'm talking.

"But I know we have to do this," I say.

"How do you know that?"

I pace around the garden. "Because it's helped other lakes. How can we just sit around and do nothing? We have to try something!"

He laughs, throwing his head back a little. "You remind me of my grandfather. He was one of the town founders, you know. He fought for a lot of things he believed in. Quite a maverick."

"Really?"

"Yep." He stands, looks toward the lake. "I'm more than willing to help."

"You are?"

He nods. "And if I'm not mistaken, most of the supplies you need are right here in the store."

"I know, I figured that. But the thing is . . . I don't have any money at the moment."

Suddenly, my phone starts buzzing like crazy. It's Maya, several rapid texts in a row. "I ran into Zach. He told me about Jess! What's going on? Did your dad find her? Where are you? Zach thought maybe you were going to ALDEN'S!! Are you there? WHAT IS HAPPENING? Are you OKAY? Please tell me you're okay. Please respond ASAP."

I reply: "Yes, I'm at Alden's. I'm okay."

"Annalise," Mr. Alden says when I click off my phone. "It would be my pleasure to donate the supplies."

I'm about to say no, I can't let him do that, when Zach, Maya, Henry, and Tyler burst into the garden.

"We were out front," Maya says, grinning and hugging me. "I'm so proud of you. This is huge, Annalise. Huge!"

I nod, folding the handkerchief and sliding it into my pocket.

“You came in here,” Maya whispers in my ear. “Now you can do anything.”

As quiet and calm as it was before, now it’s a blur of noise and color. Maya’s red T-shirt and silver sandals. Henry poking his lightsaber into a pot and Tyler shouting “Hi-ya!” and jabbing the trellis.

Maya tells the boys to stop acting like crazy people, and Zach gently guides them away from the pot and the trellis.

“But I have to fight the bad bacteria!” Tyler yells, leaping onto the bench. Henry joins him, and they wave their lightsabers in the air.

“Guys! There’s no bacteria here,” Maya says, rolling her eyes. Then to me: “They’re obsessed.”

Mr. Alden goes into the store. He comes back a few minutes later, carrying a stack of empty plastic trays, the kind that flowers come in, like the geraniums Dad and I planted in the window boxes outside the office.

“These should do just fine,” he says. “Now, let’s talk about plants.”

Zach takes one of the trays and turns it over. There are several holes, perfect for dangling roots. “Wait. Are these for the floating islands?”

“Indeed,” Mr. Alden replies. “Annalise mentioned what you need. I believe I have some varieties that would work.”

"You can't give us all that for free," I protest.

He brushes a hand at me.

Zach pulls a twenty-dollar bill from his pocket and offers it to Mr. Alden. "Will this cover it?" Mr. Alden doesn't take it.

"What are you guys doing?" Henry asks.

Zach grins at him. "We're going to fight the bad bacteria."

"Really?" Henry jumps from the bench and lays his lightsaber on the ground. "Can I help?"

Tyler leaps off too, almost knocking his brother over. "Don't forget about me!" He tugs Maya's shorts. "I'm tired of the park."

Mr. Alden still hasn't accepted Zach's money, so he stuffs the bill back into his pocket. "If it's okay with Annalise," Zach says.

"We're making them now?" I say. "Here?"

Mr. Alden shrugs. "Why not? I don't exactly have many customers at the moment."

They all look at me, and I get a pang of guilt. My sister's somewhere in Madison and Mom and Dad are freaked out, but I'm only thinking about Renn.

"Give me a sec." I pull out my phone and text Mom. "Anything?"

She replies no, that Dad found the location for the audition, but so far, no Jess.

"Do you want me to come back?"

"Are you still doing what you needed to do?"

I glance at Maya, the boys, then Zach and Mr. Alden, all waiting for me. "Yes."

"I'm okay," Mom says. "I'll let you know the minute I hear something."

"You're sure?"

"Yes."

I slide my phone into my pocket. "Let's do this!"

Tyler claps and Henry shouts, "Woo-hoo!"

Maya says to Mr. Alden, "I have some money too. From babysitting these little monsters." She ruffles their hair. "Actually, you guys aren't so bad."

"We'll address the finances later," he answers. "For now, let's get to work."

"Are you sure you want to do this, Mr. Alden?" I ask. "I don't want you to get in trouble."

"I'll take the risk. You gotta stir things up once in a while, right?"

He goes inside again, then drags out a big plastic bag of soil. He cuts it open and tells Henry and Tyler to lay out the plastic trays on the ground. Mr. Alden hands each of them a plastic scooper. "You'll be the fillers."

"We're the fillers," Tyler repeats, beaming.

Zach and I go into the store to look through the plants. There are irises and several ferns, as well as some grasses and reeds. Zach's consulting his phone, then pointing to the plants we should use. I carry them out to the garden.

The boys scoop and pat down a layer of soil in each of the seven trays laid out on the walkway in the middle of the garden. Zach and I add the plants; then Maya gently works the roots through the holes. She insisted on wearing gardening gloves, and Mr. Alden handed her a pair. "I prefer them too." He grimaced. "Worms. Can't stand 'em."

With every plant I secure into the soil, it's as though the very air in the garden is shifting. Getting lighter. And Mrs. Alden is looking over my shoulder, smiling.

We work steadily for a while. Mr. Alden brings out bottles of water and a bag of pretzels, which we devour. Maya starts singing "Down by the Bay" and we come up with rhymes, each one sillier than the last. Tyler ends the song with "Have you ever seen a goose kissing a moose?" and we're laughing so hard, we can hardly finish.

But eventually, we've used all the soil and plants. The trays are full.

I step back to admire the seven small, beautiful islands. Each one has a slightly different variety of plants, but they all look ready to go to work.

"What now?" I ask.

"We should set them afloat at night," Zach suggests. "Less risk of someone stopping us."

Maya raises her eyebrows. "Oooh. Dangerous. I like it."

"How about we meet back here at nine tonight?" Mr. Alden says.

Henry crosses his arms. "That's past our bedtime!"

Maya pats his shoulder. "Sorry, bud, but you guys are going to have to miss this part."

"Noooo!" Henry wails.

My phone buzzes. It's a text from Mom: "Dad's got her. She's fine. They're on their way home."

I blow out a long breath I didn't even realize I was holding, and my voice breaks as I tell them Dad found Jess.

"Good, that's good." Maya nods, then says to the boys, "You aren't going to miss much. You did the important part."

"Can't you sneak us out?" Henry pleads. "While the 'rents are asleep."

"The *'rents*? I don't think so. No sneaking out."

"Pleeease?" Tyler says.

"No way."

"Nine," Mr. Alden repeats.

I touch one of the plants. "I'll be here."

"Me too," Zach says.

Maya smiles. "Me three."

Tyler presses his palms together. "We'll behave!"

Maya shakes her head. "Nope. Final answer. And don't say a word of this to the 'rents either."

"Then it's settled," I say. Or it will be, soon.

Chapter Thirty-Two

ANNALISE

Mom and I are in the porch swing when the car pulls into the driveway. Jess's face is red and puffy, and Dad's is serious but relieved. They get out, close the doors, and quietly walk up the steps.

Jess stands in front of Mom, arms at her sides. Black blotches of mascara are dotted underneath her eyes, and an uneven coating of makeup is streaked with dried tears. She's wearing jeans and a white tank top.

"Mom. Before you say anything, I want to say I'm sorry. I'm really, really sorry. I won't do anything like that ever again."

Mom sighs. "Sounds like you had some time to think during the ride home."

"No." Her shoulders sag. "I started thinking as soon as we left. And don't blame Amy, or her mom. I told them you said I could go." She perches on the arm of a chair. "Dad's already heard all this, but it was terrible. We waited in line for hours. There were thousands of kids at the audition and they were only picking ten. When I was almost at the front, I put the coins down on a table for a minute so I could fill out the form. When I looked back, they were gone. I was going to ask Amy's mom for some money but I just . . . couldn't. So I didn't even get to try out." She glances at me. "I'll pay you back, I swear. Every single cent."

Jess sniffles. "When Amy finally got in the room, she sang for, like, a second, and then they said, 'Thank you.' Thank you for what? She said they barely listened to her and didn't even look up. If this is how they cast movies, forget it."

Dad drops onto the porch steps, runs a hand back through his hair. "I don't think you can sum up the entire industry from this one experience, but it sounds like you got a good look at what goes on. And learned a few things. So maybe this wasn't all bad."

Jess kind of laughs. "The dumbest thing of all is I kept thinking about *The Wizard of Oz,* and how being in a play here might not be so boring. At the end, don't they talk about, like, finding adventure in your own backyard?"

"Yeah," I say.

"If anything had happened to you"—Mom gulps—"wandering around by yourself in a big crowd like that—"

"But nothing did. Except me ending up feeling like a complete idiot for putting the coins down. And going in the first place. And . . ." She looks down. "Lying."

Jess starts to cry. I can't believe it. There are only a few times I remember her crying—the pie awards ceremony when Isabelle was announced as the winner, the day I left for kindergarten, and when Dad took her "pet" frog back to the lake.

My sister crawls into Mom's lap, tucks in her legs and curls up, her head on Mom's shoulder. Mom strokes her hair and murmurs while she rocks the swing. "You're okay now. You're home."

They stay like that for a few minutes; then Dad hands Jess a tissue. She dabs her eyes and blows her nose. "Better?" Dad asks.

Jess nods, her eyes round and big. "Are you going to ground me? Or take away my phone?"

Mom looks over at Dad, then shakes her head. "I don't think we have to. I think you understand."

She hiccups. "Good, because I want to comment on their social media pages about how bad this whole thing was. People should know. And, really? A musical about an alien invasion? What are they thinking? That's so going to flop."

Dad laughs. "Maybe one day you'll make your own movie."

Jess pushes away from Mom and sits up. She narrows her eyes. "Yeah, maybe I will."

We stay on the porch for a while, the sky turning a deeper blue, until Jess says, "I'm starving! I need pizza, right now!"

Dad cracks up. "We all do."

Pizza is ordered and eaten, the table is wiped off, the dishwasher is filled. Mom and Dad slowly climb the stairs, saying they're exhausted. Jess says she's going up too.

I watch the clock above the fireplace, hanging near the family picture and the old cabin key, slowly ticking toward eight-forty, when I plan to leave.

It's taking forever.

Finally.

As quietly as possible, I put on my shoes and slip out the front door. A streetlight shines a strong beam on the path ahead. I haven't even reached the sidewalk when I hear a whisper: "Where are you going?"

Jess is standing on the porch, her face shadowed by the big tree in our front yard.

"I have to do something," I say. "Go back upstairs."

"What is it?"

"Just . . . something."

"You don't want to tell me, do you?"

"No, it's not that." I pull out my phone to look at the

time. Eight-forty-two. "Jess, I really have to go or I'll be late."

She stands there, blinking. "Are you going to steal a pie?" She takes a step forward, out of the shadow, into the light, toward me. "Because, you know, I'm really good at stealing pies."

A smile spreads across my face. She remembers. "You didn't steal it, I did."

"But I was your accomplice."

"You were."

We look at each other, and the sweet taste of Isabelle's pink lemonade pie floods into my mouth.

"Get some shoes," I say. "Fast."

I scribble a quick note for Mom and Dad—*Don't worry, we're okay*—in case they wake up.

Jess is back out in two seconds; then she's scurrying to keep up with me on the sidewalk. "So where *are* we going?" she whispers.

"Alden's."

"What!"

"Shhh."

"Why *there*?"

"We're saving the lake."

"From that algae stuff?"

"Yes. Long story, but I made these floating plant islands today with Mr. Alden and Maya and Henry and

Tyler and Zach, and we're putting them out on the lake tonight."

"Wait. Back up. You went into *Alden's*?"

"I did."

"And talked to Mr. Alden?"

"Uh-huh."

She claps a hand over her mouth. "I can't believe it."

"Neither can I. But I had to. For . . ."

"For who? You mean, to save the lake?"

"Yes. C'mon."

I start to run. Jess catches up with me. We jog side by side toward Main, hearing only our breath and the rustling of the trees. We reach Alden's exactly at nine.

The store is dark, but a single spotlight glimmers on the flamingos in the window, making them look eerie, like they come alive at night when no one's around. I quietly open the door, and we hurry to the back garden. Mr. Alden's there, with Zach. They're examining the plants on the islands.

"Hi," I whisper, then tip my head toward Jess. "My sister's coming with us. JessiKa, with a capital *K*."

Zach and Mr. Alden nod. Zach says, "Hey."

She shrugs. "Actually, I've thought it over, and I'm going back to Jess. For now."

"Good," I say. "I like Jess better."

Maya appears, out of breath. "Sorry I'm a little late."

Mr. Alden looks at us. "Ready?"

"Yes," I answer.

We each take an island, and Zach and I carry two. We walk out of the store in a silent line. Mr. Alden puts his island down to lock the door. Then the five of us cross the empty street together and walk to the end, where it stops at the lake. When we reach the shore, we set the islands down, across from the algae patch.

The sky is completely dark now, with an umbrella of stars and a half-moon partly obscured by a cloud. Maya turns on the flashlight on her phone.

"No lights," Zach whispers.

"I agree," Mr. Alden says. "It's best not to attract attention."

Maya flips off the light.

"So we just put them in the water?" I say quietly.

"I've been reading everything I can find," Zach replies. "They're supposed to be anchored, but we don't have the means to do that. I think it'll be okay to just set them afloat for now. They should settle in a spot and start working. Hopefully."

Jess bends toward one of the islands.

"Just a moment." Mr. Alden reaches into his pocket. He takes out some leaves and hands one to each of us. "Sage. My grandfather grew it. Since he was one of the founders of the town and worked his entire life to protect our land and our lake, I thought we should add a sage leaf to each island for good luck."

I hold the leaf to my nose, inhale its mysterious mixture of sharp and sweet, then tuck it into one of the islands. "Was your grandfather the one who named Sage Street?"

"He was indeed."

I smile. Of course he was.

Zach, Maya, Jess, and Mr. Alden add the leaves too. We spread out, as close to the water as possible. One by one, we lean forward and set our islands onto the lake. I give mine a gentle push, sending it on its way.

Moonlight trickles across the seven islands, making them look like miniature, lit-up fairy gardens. A few of them rotate slowly, as the insects hum and the trees crackle. Somewhere, an owl hoots. We stand there watching for a while, not saying anything.

Maya says finally, "This is a mitzvah."

"What's that?" Jess asks.

"Doing something good."

"Yes," I say, imagining the roots dangling underwater, gathering up the algae. Invisible. Strong.

Zach sighs. "We'll see what happens."

Mr. Alden nods. "As with most things."

"They look so . . . small," Maya says. "How will they possibly get all the algae?"

Jess huffs a little. “Just because something’s small doesn’t mean it can’t do big things.”

I smile at her. She smiles back and reaches for my hand. “I’m tired,” she says.

I wrap my fingers around hers. “Me too.”

Zach says goodbye and walks toward his cabin. Mr. Alden crosses the street and gets into his car. Maya, Jess, and I head home.

When we get there, Maya slips through our yard to hers. Jess pauses on our porch steps. “Annalise.”

I stop, look at her.

“I still want to leave one day, you know.”

“I know.”

I crumple the note I left for Mom and Dad and we tiptoe up the stairs together. At my bedroom door, she digs in her pocket and pulls something out. A dime.

“I found it in the bathroom at the audition,” she whispers. “Ten cents toward what I owe you.” She hands it to me and sneaks into her room.

I go into my room and drop the coin into a crooked ceramic bowl I made in art last year. It lands with a clink. The start of something new.

Chapter Thirty-Three

TRU

I heard Renn calling out to me, but I chose to turn my back. I could have helped. I could have carried the woman back in my current. But instead, I chose to carry her away.

The canoe rocked and almost tipped over. She dropped the oar. She clutched the sides of the narrow boat, raised her face to the dark sky and began to cry.

I pushed the canoe toward my eastern bank. At least I did that.

She slipped into my water, grabbed onto the earth and pulled herself up on dry land. She crumpled into a heap and laid there for hours.

The sun rose. Renn told me about the baby. But it was too late. The woman was gone.

I need to apologize. To Renn, for not listening, and for never speaking of that night. To the woman, who was lost. To the girl who was left behind.

It's time to forgive.

I see the islands they have set afloat. Beautiful, tiny keys of hope, much stronger and more powerful than they appear. They have the ability to heal. To make things right again.

I start by giving them my blessing.

Chapter Thirty-Four

ANNALISE

I dream of roots floating in the water, and Renn's whispers and waves and words. I dream there's no more algae and our magical islands sail away in the breeze, helped along by the breath of water spirits. Lake mermaids.

A text from Zach jolts me awake: "Trouble. Get to the lake ASAP."

The sun's just poking through my window. I roll out of bed, rush into Jess's room, and shake her shoulder. "Get up. We have to go."

She rubs her eyes, groans. "What time is it?"

"Seven-fifteen."

She puts her pillow over her head. "Too early."

I pull it off. "Zach texted. Something happened at the lake."

She bolts up. "What?"

"Shhh. I don't know."

Mom and Dad's bedroom door is closed, surprisingly. I quickly get dressed and scribble a note that we left early. Jess and I run to the lake.

Two people from the health department are talking with Zach. Someone must have spotted the floating islands early this morning and called them. I had a feeling this would happen. I just didn't think it would be this soon.

"Should I text Maya?" Jess asks.

"Yes." I hand her my phone.

When I reach them, I realize it's Kim and Keith, from the meeting at the library. "Let me ask you again," Keith is saying to Zach, "do you have any idea who put these out on the lake?"

Zach shakes his head, swallows, adjusts his glasses. "I don't live here. I've been staying in one of the cabins."

"These haven't been approved." Kim's rifling through papers attached to a clipboard. "I don't see anywhere on my notes where these were ordered."

Keith taps on his phone. "I'm calling Brinkley."

"Good," Kim replies. "We need to get to the bottom of this right away."

He walks a few feet away. "Brinkley? Keith here. We have a situation."

"Who's Brinkley?" Jess asks.

Kim's still flipping through the papers. "Our boss. Head of the department. Maybe I missed an email?"

Zach looks at me over Kim's shoulder. "What should we do?" he mouths.

I scan the islands, drifting serenely on the algae. I swear I can smell the sage leaves. What would Mr. Alden's grandfather do?

I clear my throat. "You didn't miss an email."

Kim glances up, tilts her head. "Excuse me?"

"It was me. I put the floating islands on the lake."

Kim lowers her clipboard. "You did?"

I nod. "Yes. Last night."

Jess folds her arms defiantly across her chest and rises up on her tiptoes. "I also put one out there. So if you're gonna arrest her, arrest me too."

"Keith?" Kim calls. "I think we've found our culprits."

Keith says into the phone, "Okay, see you in a bit," then walks back over to us. Kim points to me and Jess.

"They did it," she states firmly, as if he should handcuff us on the spot.

"Brinkley's on his way," Keith tells her. He shoves his phone into his shorts pocket. "You girls wanna explain?"

"I'm sure you've heard of floating plant islands," I say in a rush. "How their roots soak up the toxins? They've worked on other lakes. We—I mean, I—made them and put them out last night."

He frowns. "Without contacting my office?"

"We did. My dad called, but they said—"

"He didn't speak to me."

"I couldn't just—" My voice trembles and I try to steady it. "I couldn't just keep waiting for the bloom to go away. Do nothing. This is my lake. It was hurting. It was . . . dying."

"It's *our* lake," Jess pipes in.

Zach raises his hand. "Okay, I admit it, Officer. I'm guilty too. I was a part of this."

Suddenly, Maya's standing at my side, with Henry and Tyler next to her. "You might as well add me in too," she says.

"And me!" Henry shouts.

"Don't forget about me!" Tyler echoes. "I helped! I put the soil in the trays! It was so much more fun than going to the park."

Keith raises his eyebrows. "You kids didn't have the authority to do this. I'm not exactly sure how we're going to handle it. Brinkley's on his way. He'll make the call."

"Brinkley?" Maya asks.

"The man in charge."

"I look forward to speaking with him," Jess says, crossing her arms. My sister gives me a sneaky smile.

Kim and Keith walk toward the water, talking to each other quietly. Maya pulls out her phone and starts texting. The boys grab two sticks and begin digging a hole in the dirt. Where are their lightsabers?

Zach edges over to me. "This isn't good. I'm worried. Is there a way we can get in touch with Mr. Alden?"

My hands are shaking and my heart is filling up, flooding over. They don't get it. What if they rip out the islands? Then we did all this for nothing.

"It's too early for the store to be open," I say. "And I don't have his number or anything."

"Right. But maybe we can—"

"Wait." I look down. Zach's wearing red canvas slip-ons. "You got new shoes?"

"While you were at Alden's yesterday, I went to Castaway and found these. No laces. No knots. Whaddya think?"

I smile. He glances toward his cabin. "My dad came too."

"Really?"

"Yeah. He bought a tweed cap. He thinks it makes him look more like a writer."

"Does it?"

Zach laughs. "Well, he's on page thirty-two."

Maya's still texting, and Jess is standing next to her,

looking at her phone too. Are they even worried about what's going on?

I turn back to Zach. "What do you think is going to happen when Brinkley gets here?"

"I'm not feeling optimistic, to be honest."

"We have to make them understand."

He sighs. "Adults don't usually listen to kids."

I think of Mr. Alden. "Sometimes they do."

"I'm crossing my fingers they'll give us a chance," Zach says.

I spot a moving blur of pink in the distance, on Main Street, getting closer and closer. The blur comes into focus. Jean from the movie theater is wearing pink shorts, a pink top, and her pink rhinestone glasses, and is marching in our direction. Right behind her is Toni from Castaway.

Maya nudges Jess. "Keep going. Text more people." Jess's fingers are flying across her screen, and then my phone too. "I'm on it."

Within minutes, the shore fills with more people. Mayor Greg, Maya's parents, Henry and Tyler's mom, several kids from my class last year, as well as Maya's and Jess's classes. Even Isabelle, the pie champion, is here.

"What's happening?" Zach asks me, shading his eyes and scanning the group.

"I don't know."

The few guests from the cabins make their way over, including Sophie and her grandparents. More shop owners arrive. Mom and Dad walk up, looking confused, and Vera, who doesn't look at all confused. Last to get here is Mr. Alden. And then, coming out of cabin 8 is a man in a tweed cap.

Everyone's talking about the plant islands. Asking questions, pointing to them, and reading on their phones. An electric buzz is pulsing through the crowd.

Dad comes over to me. "Let me take a wild guess. You had something to do with this?"

"Dad. The lake is in serious trouble. How could I not do anything?"

"My daughters seem to think they can just take it upon themselves to—" Dad starts, then stops as Mr. Alden taps his shoulder.

"I'm in on this too, Jay," he says. "So whatever you're about to tell Annalise, you might as well tell me too."

Dad opens his mouth, then shuts it as a loud voice booms, "Make way, please. Thanks very much. Comin' through."

The tallest man I've pretty much ever seen is standing next to me. Or rather, over me. He's got to be close to seven feet. I look way, way up as he extends a hand. "Brinkley Wilson," he says, shaking mine. He's wearing a denim shirt, not a brown one. On it, a green badge says HEALTH OFFICER.

"So what do we have here?" he asks.

"Floating plant islands," I say weakly. "You've heard of them?"

Jess is pushing her way through the crowd. She marches right up to Brinkley and offers her hand. "Jess Oliver," she says. He shakes it.

Brinkley eyes me. "And you are?"

"Annalise. Annalise Oliver."

"My sister," Jess says, then gestures to Zach. "Our colleague can bring you up to speed."

Zach squeaks, "Me?" and Jess nods.

Zach explains how we made the islands and set them afloat last night. "It'll take some time, and we know this is only part of the answer, but it's a start. It should help lessen, then eventually clean up the algal bloom. This method has been used successfully on other lakes. In Montana, Illinois, and China . . ."

Zach's voice drifts off as Brinkley goes over to one of the islands near the shore. He studies it, then looks back at us. "I believe these are anchored to a lake bed. And have a filter to attract the microbes."

"Yes, they should be, but we didn't have the materials to do that." Zach glances at me. "We thought it would be better to just get the process started."

Jess strides toward Brinkley, little tufts of her hair wafting up. She taps his arm. An elf bothering a giant. He turns and looks down at her.

"I hope you're not planning to remove them," she says. "Because I'm doing a documentary about this whole thing."

Brinkley raises an eyebrow. "You are."

"Uh-huh. You probably haven't heard of the Renn Lake Elementary School Film Club because I'm starting it in the fall, but I'm making our first movie. *The Magic of Floating Plant Islands.* We start filming today, in fact. I'm the director. It's a big job."

"Is that right?" Brinkley asks, smiling.

"Yes." Jess does a very small, very controlled foot stomp. Then she motions to the crowd with both hands, urging them forward.

Everyone moves toward the lake and something amazing happens. They spread out and form a human barrier in front of the islands.

"This is our lake," Jess announces. "And the islands are staying right where they are."

Far, far off in the distance, where the river connects to Renn, I hear a low rumble, then a gushing. It almost sounds like applause.

A few beats of silence; then Brinkley nods. "I admire

your enthusiasm, and your commitment. I'm pretty blown away by it, to be honest."

I'm waiting for the but: *But they have to come out. But you made them wrong. But you shouldn't have done this. But you're in trouble.*

There are no buts.

Instead, Brinkley motions to Kim and Keith. "We need to apply for a permit for these anchors. We're going to need . . ." He turns and counts the islands. "Seven."

My heart leaps a mile in the air. "They can stay?"

"For now. Let's give these babies some time. See what they can do. We'll keep an eye on them." He scans the lake. "We could use a few more, in fact. It's a pretty big bloom."

Tyler wiggles his way toward Brinkley. "Me and my brother can do it. We can make some more."

Brinkley crouches. "Terrific, son. We need people like you because there's a lot of work to do. Not just the islands, but changing some things so this doesn't happen again. Are you up to the job?"

"I am, sir!" Tyler salutes him.

Henry goes to stand next to Tyler as Maya appears at my side. She's beaming at the boys. "I never thought I'd say this, but they're good kids, you know?"

"Where are their lightsabers?"

"They said they didn't need 'em today, that the plants would blow up the bad bacteria."

I laugh. "I hope so. You and Jess were texting everyone? Thanks for getting the word out."

"You're welcome." She gives me my phone. "Is your sister really making a documentary, or was she bluffing? Because if she was, that was excellent acting. I totally bought it."

"You never know with Jess."

Zach is next to Brinkley, and they're gesturing to the islands. Kim and Keith are talking on their phones. My sister is by Mom and Dad, and I hear her ask them where our old video camera is, and if it still works. Maybe she is serious about the documentary. The crowd is breaking up, people fanning out like streamers.

Henry calls out to Maya and she jogs toward him. I sense someone behind me and turn to see Mr. Alden. "Looks like we've got more islands to make," he says.

I take hold of my necklace, slide the tiny house around the chain, and let it drop back against my skin. "Yes, we do."

"So I'll see you soon?" He winks at me. "Not in twelve years?"

I smile. "Not in twelve years."

"You let me know when. I'll be here."

"Okay. I will."

He starts to walk away.

"Wait, Mr. Alden?"

He looks back.

"Thank you. For the supplies. And helping us." *And the handkerchief,* I want to add, but I can't. "I don't know if I said it yesterday."

He gives me a little wave. "No need." He walks toward Main, arms swinging. I watch until he reaches his store, those goofy flamingos shining in the window, unlocks the door, and goes inside.

Chapter Thirty-Five

ANNALISE

The islands have been on the lake for a week, and every day I've checked the bloom but it looks about the same. I know they take time to work, but still. I wish there was some small sign.

The Thought Wall's become a get-well message board for Renn, with notes like: *Hope the islands work* and *Wishing the lake a speedy recovery.* Once one person started doing it, everyone joined in, and now the wall is covered with positive messages. One note even says: *We miss you, Renn Lake!*

I miss Renn too. It's been a long time since I heard anything. We made three new islands at Alden's and put them out on the water. I have faith in the islands, but I worry that the bloom has done some permanent damage. I keep pushing away my biggest fear: that I'll never hear Renn again.

Mom and Dad are busier again. Their calls and emails

helped, because a scrapbooking group is here, staying in five cabins. The women said the algae didn't matter because they weren't planning on swimming or canoeing. Mom set up tables for them in the office and they've been cutting, gluing, and chattering constantly. Mom's making them lemonade and snacks, and admiring their creations. Maya even got Henry and Tyler involved, collecting scraps of paper to recycle and handing out pieces of tape. Mom gave them Renn Lake Rentals caps to wear, and the scrapbookers have been calling the boys their "assistants." I haven't seen their lightsabers in a while.

Dad told me a chess club booked several cabins next week for a tournament, so that should help pay some bills. "Your sister's been telling us we need a"—he made air quotes—"'social media presence,' and I think she's right. We're overdue for some upgrades around here."

"But you're not going to change the cabins into some fancy hotel, right?"

"Not on your life. But we can post pictures, upload videos, and create a hashtag." He did the hashtag symbol with his fingers.

I raised an eyebrow and smiled at him. "Who are you?"

On day eight (I'm counting), Maya, Zach, and I are hanging out on the shore. Jess is wandering around with the video camera, taking shots of the lake from different angles, and Henry and Tyler are tossing a football back and forth.

"I still can't believe they didn't take out the islands," I say.

"I know," Zach replies. "The way they were talking about Brinkley—the man in charge and all that—I thought we were goin' down. But he was the nicest."

Maya nods. "He was. This whole thing, wow. Just wow." She's threading a red ribbon around a white basket for raffle tickets at the Fourth of July Fest.

Zach pulls off his glasses, wipes sweat from the sides of his nose. I can hear the slap of the football on Henry's and Tyler's hands every time they catch it, but other than that, it's sticky quiet.

I look at the islands, one by one, floating on the green. "Zach?"

"Yeah?"

"What happened after those other lakes got rid of the algae? Everything I read only focused on how the islands worked."

"What do you mean?"

"Well, let's say the islands cure the bloom here eventually. But what if this happens again? What if more cyanobacteria form and it becomes a bloom again? What if it keeps happening, over and over?"

Zach stretches out his legs, crosses them at the ankle. "Yeah. To be honest, the islands are kind of a Band-Aid."

"Why?" Maya asks.

"To really tackle this, you gotta take care of what caused the bloom in the first place. Brinkley and I were talking about how hard it is to control the polluted runoff that gets into the water."

"Exactly," I say. "Remember how Keith said at the meeting—'down the drain, the driveway, into the sewer.' It all ends up in the lake."

Maya puts the basket down. "How do you change that?"

"Everyone has to help," Zach says. "Stop fertilizing your lawn as much, and don't use pesticides. Even washing your car in the driveway can send junk into the water."

"Some people are careful, but others don't bother, right?" Maya says.

Zach nods. "That's how it always is. You should see what people in my apartment building throw away when it could be recycled. It's so sad."

We're all silent for a few minutes; then Maya narrows her eyes. "I've got an idea."

"What?" I ask.

She crosses her arms. "Let's set up an information booth at the fest. Then everyone in town will know what to do."

I leap up. "That's a great idea!"

Maya starts counting off on her fingers. "We'll make a three-panel display board, hand out brochures, maybe even have something interactive. We should put a cup of algae on the table so everyone can see how gross it is up close. People can sign a pledge to do their part. We can do a game for kids—"

"Let's have a rain barrel," Zach interrupts.

"Sure. Whatever that is."

"It's a container to collect rainwater at your house so it doesn't wash into the lake. Then you use it to water your grass and plants."

"Maybe we can raise money for permeable pavement too," I add.

Maya grins. "It's like you guys are speaking another language."

"I read about them," I say. "They replace the concrete in sidewalks and driveways with something else, like crushed-up glass bottles. Rain goes right into the ground and won't run into the lake."

"How cool is that?" Maya says.

I wave my arms. "We're going to need streamers, string lights, and balloons. Maybe a disco ball if we can hang it somewhere! I want everyone to come to this booth."

She laughs. "Sure, why not."

Jess comes over. "What's going on?"

"We're doing an information booth at the fest," I announce. "About what people can do so the lake never gets an algal bloom again!"

"Awesome!" Jess holds up the camera. "I'll be there."

Maya texts her parents and they love the idea. Zach pulls the twenty from his pocket and says he can help buy supplies. "And I'll use some of my babysitting money," Maya adds. "The 'rents will be very proud."

"I'm broke," I moan.

Jess looks at the ground and pushes the dirt with the toe of her shoe. "You have ten cents."

"No worries," Maya says. "You can pay us back."

We rush to the office and tell Mom and Dad our plan. It seems like all the scrapbookers are listening too. Mom and Dad also love the idea, and offer us an empty cabin to use for our preparations. Mom hands me the key for cabin 10. "Let us know if you need anything."

As soon as we get inside, Tyler and Henry start jumping on the bed. "Get down, you two!" Maya shouts. "This is serious. You told Brinkley you were up to the job." She rolls her eyes.

Maya launches into maximum planning mode, taking charge and assigning everyone projects and tasks. We make a list of materials, then walk to the only grocery store in town. Thankfully, we find everything.

We spend the entire week researching and making

items for the booth. Maya brings in a dry-erase board and props it against a wall of the cabin. Each morning she holds a staff meeting and goes over the plan for the day. Full-steam-ahead Maya. Doing what she does best.

Zach and I work diligently on the display board, covering it with articles, website links, photos, and bulleted points on what people can do. Henry and Tyler make a spin-the-wheel game. Jean hears about what we're doing and donates movie passes for us to hand out to people who land on the winning space, which says RENN LAKE CHAMPION.

Jess is filming everything and interviewing us. Amy's been advising her on angles, lighting, and framing, plus singing various show tunes.

The night before the fest, Maya draws a line through the last item on the dry-erase board. "We're ready," she says. We plan to meet early the next morning to set everything up. Maya makes us get in a circle and put our hands together. Then we shout, "For the lake!"

The sun is just coming up when Jess and I get to the shore. Our table is between the kids' art area and the food tent, so I hope that's a good spot with a lot of traffic. We cover the table with Mom's blue tablecloth. I stand up the display board and Maya fans out the brochures we designed and printed at her house. Zach dips a clear plastic cup into the lake, comes back, and puts it on the table. Still as thick and green as ever. Are the roots even helping? Next to the cup, Zach places a clipboard with sheets of paper for people to sign their names, committing to do their part to make Renn Lake an algae-free zone from now on.

We couldn't get an actual rain barrel, but we added a section about them to the display board, explaining how they work. Maya puts the donation bucket in the center of the table. On the front, it says HELP US GET PERMEABLE PAVEMENT. She drops in the first dollar.

Henry and Tyler add their spin-the-wheel game to one end of the table, then stand behind it. "I get the first person," Henry says.

"How come you do?" Tyler replies. "That's not fair."

"Fine, we race for it, okay? Winner goes first."

The boys dart away from the table; then Henry points. "To that tree and back." He asks Maya to say ready, set, go. She does, and they're off. Henry wins, and it looks like Tyler's trying not to cry.

"Tyler," Maya says quickly. "You get to help Annalise with the streamers."

"Ha," Tyler snorts, then grabs the tape from my hand. It's the roll my teacher gave me on the last day of school, as a reminder to tape up something that's torn and go on. It's time for me to use it.

Tyler and I undo the red, white, and blue streamers and loop them around the table. We put a piece of tape every few inches until the roll is empty; then we stand back and look. "Good," he says. "People will like it."

I curl a strand of string lights around the display board and tie some balloons on the table legs. Perfect.

Mr. Alden heads toward our table. He offers me a small bowl filled with wrapped red-and-white peppermint candies. "Starlight mints," he says. "People like a little something sweet."

"Thanks." I make space for it as he looks everything over. "Nice job," he says, then pulls something from his shirt pocket. A handkerchief. This one has a tiny yellow bird on it. He blots his forehead, then squeezes it in his hand.

During the fest, our booth is constantly crowded. At one point, there's even a line of people waiting to talk to us! Henry and Tyler are beaming over their game, which everyone wants to try, and people are actually dropping coins and dollars into the donation bucket. Zach never seems to get tired of answering scientific questions, and Maya is hanging back and taking it all in.

Jess, who's been filming all day, marches over when

the sky begins to darken. "Once again, Isabelle got first in the pie competition. How is it possible that she's won for three years in a row? The only explanation is that it's fixed."

"Whatever," I say. "We have more important things to do."

She looks over everything on the table. "You know what, you're right. We do. I have, like, ten hours of video."

"Is it all going into the documentary?"

"Oh, no. I have a lot of editing to do. Amy's going to help. It'll take me the rest of the summer." She tilts her head. "What are you going to do? The cabins are still kinda quiet."

I peek inside the bucket. "I think I'm going to . . . keep this going. Continue talking to people. Knock on doors. Make sure we take care of the lake."

She gives me a thumbs-up. "I gotta go. Amy's singing on the main stage in a few minutes."

"Oh, cool."

"Later!" She slings the strap around her shoulder and runs off, the camera bobbing against her hip.

Zach's standing in back of the booth, straightening things up. A breeze ruffles the brochures, and he clamps a hand on the top one. With the other, he pulls his phone from his pocket and smiles, then starts texting. When he's done, as he's putting his phone down, I steal a glance. A long message to someone named Ryan. My heart bursts a little.

A crowd gathers by the food tent. I hear Amy's voice ring out, and a few minutes later, applause. She really does have a good voice.

There's one last peppermint candy in the bowl. I unwrap it and pop it into my mouth. It's sharp and sweet, like the sage leaves. Like me and Jess. Maybe like everything.

I sit in front of the table as the first round of fireworks lights up the sky above the lake. Zach comes around and sits next to me. He's leaving tomorrow.

We watch the bursts and explosions, trickles and sizzles, and listen to the oohs and aahs.

"I have to tell you something," he says.

"What?"

"I'm not going to try to be a different person anymore."

I tap the toe of my shoe against his red canvas one. "Good choice."

He has such a great smile.

Chapter Thirty-Six

ANNALISE

It's Labor Day. School starts on Wednesday. The air feels different, like it always does at the end of summer: a little cooler, a little tired.

Mom and Dad are at the cabins, closing them up for the off-season. Mom took down all the notes from the Thought Wall, then wrote one herself and stuck it up there. *We survived,* it says. *See you next year. A new and improved #RennLakeRentals!*

Next June will be my thirteenth found day. I'll be a . . . teenager.

I finish packing my backpack, arranging notebooks and my pencil case. I go outside and sit on the porch step; then, for some reason, I get the urge to ride my bike. I haven't ridden it all summer. I wheel it out of the shed, brush off some dust, and bring it around to the front of the house.

Even though I'm too big for it now, like the swings, I

pedal through town, past the shops and toward the lake. But instead of going to Renn, I turn and take the road that heads toward the river. The wind is blowing my curls and my knees are practically smacking into my stomach, but I keep riding. I've never gone this far before but something's pushing me onward.

I pass the part where the mouth of the river meets Renn, then ride a while longer. Finally, I slow down and hop off my bike. I've only seen the river from a distance, from the window of a car or a bus, when we've gone on school field trips. But now, I drop my bike, go up to the water, and sit on the bank.

I wonder if I'll be able to hear the river too. I wait and listen, but there's no sound. Suddenly, something pops up. A small face with slick, dark fur and brown eyes, looking right at me. It's an otter, bobbing in the current. It seems to tip its head a little, as if it's studying me; then, with another splash, it dives below. I've looked on a map, and I know the Tru River goes north for miles. How far will the otter swim? I watch to see if its head will pop up again, but I don't spot it anywhere.

The river is calm, not what I expected. I thought I'd see a swift current, maybe even raging waters. But it feels sort of . . . content.

I stand, brush off my shorts, and get on my bike. Maybe

there is a reason for everything, even if you don't know it. Maybe things end up how they're supposed to be.

When I get to Main, I stop in front of Alden's. He's changed the window display to get ready for autumn—curled leaves and glittery pumpkins and scattered acorns. His displays are definitely getting better.

I go across to the lake, then leave my bike on the shore and walk toward the water. I promised Zach I'd text him if I hear something. And he promised to let me know how it's going in high school.

There are tiny bubbly openings here and there in the green, dotted among the islands, and I'm hopeful. "Renn?" I whisper.

Quiet. But not a terrible quiet. An expectant, better kind of quiet. But no words yet.

Jess is racing toward me. "There you are! I've been looking for you everywhere!"

"What's wrong?"

"Nothing's wrong. Something excellent happened." She jumps up and down. "Are you ready? It's *amazing*! They want to interview us for the *news*!"

"Like, a TV station?"

"Yes!"

"Seriously?"

"Yeah, from Madison! They called Mom. They heard

about everything we're doing, and my documentary, and they want to do a story on us!"

"Wow! When?"

"Not sure. We have to work that out." She looks at my bike. "Where were you, by the way?"

"I rode out to the river."

"Why? That's far."

"I don't know . . . I just wanted to."

"You can be really weird sometimes."

I smile. "So can you."

She sighs. "Didn't Mom and Dad get you that bike for your ninth found day?"

"Yeah."

"Annalise . . . ?"

"What?"

"Can we be done with found day? I hate it."

"Oh, really, I couldn't tell." I roll my eyes.

"It's not just the two celebrations, and double cupcakes, it's just . . ."

"You know what? I hate it too."

"Wait, you do?"

"Yeah."

She crosses her arms. "Then let's get rid of it! It's old news, what do we need it for?"

"Because Mom and Dad love it?"

"Maybe we can tell them to call it something else."

"Like . . . ?"

She looks me in the eyes. "I've been thinking about this. A lot. Found day's just about what happened to you when you were a baby, but if we call it *sister day,* it's about how it is now. What do you say?"

I grab her hand. "I say it sounds as perfect as pink lemonade pie."

"Ha! Good. Done." She grins. "Let's keep the cupcakes, though."

"Definitely."

Jess points to the office. "Let's go tell Mom and Dad right now."

"You go ahead. I'll be right there."

"Okay." She marches toward the office, her tufts of hair rising and falling with each step. She goes inside, and I get a glimpse of her through the window talking and gesturing to Mom and Dad. And just like that, I know found day is gone. Because of Jess. My sister.

I turn back, look at all the magical, beautiful floating islands.

"Renn?"

And then the whisper comes. Barely a sound. I don't know if it's in my head or radiating from the water, but I hear it.

The answer is here. It always was.

After

RENN

The summer has come and gone. It was not quite what I expected.

Life is like that.

I am old. Very old. There are some things I have learned along the way.

They are simple things that stay with you, solid and safe under your skin. When they are needed, they rise to the surface.

Opposite forces exist for a reason.

Out of something bad often comes something good.

Answers can always be found.

And now Tru and I are about to play. There are fish to be counted. There is air to breathe and there are people to love. A girl who listens.

There is so much.

FYI

Hi, this is Zach. Annalise asked me to tell you some cool stuff about lakes and rivers, stormwater runoff, algal blooms, and floating plant islands.

So, here goes.

LAKES

People say *amazing* a lot. But lakes are *really* amazing. Compared to oceans, lakes are small players, but they have a big impact.

Our planet has millions of lakes. You can find them on every continent and in all kinds of environments. Many of them were formed by melting glaciers thousands of years ago. I live by Lake Michigan. It's so big and stretches so far, it's hard to believe it's not an ocean.

Lakes and ponds cover less than four percent of the earth's surface. That may not sound like a lot, but they have a crucial job. Carbon is an element that's the basis of all forms of life on earth. Lakes cycle carbon between the surface of the water and the atmosphere, which helps regulate the earth's global temperature and the amount of carbon dioxide in the air. Lakes also hold carbon in decaying layers of organic muck at their bottoms. They bury way more carbon than oceans do! And they provide a home to a wide variety of organisms, from plants to animals, fish, reptiles, and insects.

Lakes, like people, go through different life stages—being born, maturing, getting old, and finally (sadly) dying. All lakes, even the largest ones, will slowly disappear as their basins fill with sediment and plant material. This happens slowly, over hundreds or thousands of years. But with climate change, this process is speeding up. *We* are speeding it up. Warmer water, less ice in the winter, and flooding—all linked to global warming—are affecting every aspect of lakes.

If you're a science geek like me and want to read more about lakes, visit National Geographic's website (nationalgeographic.org/encyclopedia/lake) and ScienceDaily (sciencedaily.com/terms/lake.htm).

RIVERS

As with lakes, countless species of fish, birds, and other animals live in and along rivers. Rivers are part of ecosystems, which connect all the plants and animals in a particular area that rely on each other and the surrounding environment for survival. Many rivers feed into lakes, like Tru and Renn. Rivers are much more than what you see when you look at the surface of the water. They provide breeding areas for migratory birds. Fish spawn in rivers. And maybe most importantly, rivers give us drinking water! The majority of the water supply in the United States comes from rivers and streams, and the health of river ecosystems directly affects the quality of the water we drink.

Many rivers are being seriously polluted and/or depleted. I don't have to tell you that breaks my heart. (More than Leo did.) (I'm a lot better now.)

Anyway, to learn more, visit americanrivers.org/threats-solutions/protecting-rivers/the-value-of-wild-river and nationalgeographic.org/encyclopedia/river.

STORMWATER RUNOFF

Runoff is the result of rain or melting snow flowing over sidewalks, streets, and driveways instead of being absorbed into the ground. The water picks up debris, chemicals, and other pollutants, which go into a lake or river. Runoff can do a lot of damage, making it difficult or impossible for plants to grow, destroying aquatic habitats, creating health hazards, and causing algal blooms. Oceans have been affected too. Red tides on Florida's coast are harmful algal blooms that produce toxins. They're happening more frequently and can last for a few weeks or longer than a year. One cause is runoff from nearby towns and farms. Many fish, birds, and sea animals, especially turtles, have died because of the tides.

We all contribute to the problem, and often we don't even realize it. But we can change our habits. Be careful about what you pour down the sink. Compost yard clippings. Use a rain barrel to collect rainwater so it doesn't wash into lakes and streams, or create a garden with plants native to your area that will soak up rainwater.

At Prairie Crossing School in Grayslake, Illinois, students raised money to replace concrete sidewalks with permeable pavement, allowing rain and snowmelt to go directly into the ground, decreasing runoff. Read about what they accomplished here: filterpave.net/prairie-crossing.

For more on what you can do, visit epa.gov/nutrientpollution/sources-and-solutions-stormwater.

ALGAL BLOOMS

I could go on and on about algal blooms and how worried I am about them. In the last few years, they've become more frequent in lakes and other bodies of water around the world. Scientists think this is related to warmer temperatures, heat waves, and other extreme weather events. The problem can be intensified by runoff, leakage from sewer systems, and other pollution.

Harmful algal blooms, also called HABs, occur in fresh water when blue-green algae grow out of control. A bloom doesn't have to be toxic to be harmful to the environment. Blooms can kill wildlife and cause beach closures. Exposure to a bloom can be dangerous for people. Pets have a higher risk of getting sick because they're smaller and may drink lake water or lick it from their coats.

If a bloom grows large enough, it can create a dead zone, covering the surface of the water and blocking sunlight, which affects species living below the surface. No oxygen gets through, and aquatic life disappears.

Scientists are studying algal blooms to figure out why they're occurring more and what the long-term effects might be. Read more on the National Oceanic and Atmospheric Administration site (oceanservice.noaa.gov/hazards/hab) and the Wisconsin Department of

Health Services site (dhs.wisconsin.gov/water/bg-algae/defined.htm).

FLOATING PLANT ISLANDS

Have you heard of something called allelopathy? It's an incredible phenomenon! It's when one plant influences the growth of another. Trees are a great example. Many use their roots to pull water from the soil away from nearby plants so the tree can survive.

This is what floating plant islands do!

The islands act as a wetland, which is a natural purifier, and clean up contaminated water. How cool is it that nature has a solution to that problem? A wetland marsh is like a giant pasta strainer. Power to the plants, right?

These islands help regulate phosphorus and nitrogen levels to improve water quality without the use of chemicals. Not only that, but the islands themselves provide a habitat for birds, reptiles, and other wildlife. In 2014, one company's floating-island design was chosen by the US State Department as one of the top innovations in water technology.

The EPA (Environmental Protection Agency) is working with the Chemehuevi and Colorado Indian Tribes to study floating islands in Lake Havasu (on the border of California and Arizona) and the Colorado River, both located within the tribes' reservations. The tribes identified native plants to use on the islands. Early results have shown promise—two months after launching the islands, the water's nutrient concentration was reduced to a safe level. If you want to read more, visit epa.gov/science matters/epa-uses-floating-vegetated-islands-remove-excess-nutrients-water.

AND SO . . .

Each positive action we take will create a better future for everyone on this planet. I'm worried, but I'm also optimistic. Kids are taking charge and forming organizations to save our earth. Here are some I know of.

The teens behind Zero Hour (thisiszerohour.org) say that time is running out to address climate change issues. They're marching, protesting, and raising awareness. You can become an ambassador in your community to educate and help come up with solutions.

Inspired by Greta Thunberg, a Swedish teen and climate activist who started Fridays for Future (fridaysfor future.org), millions of students around the world participated in demonstrations in March and September 2019 to urge adults to act. Check youthclimatestrikeus .org for more info, including the movement's platform to transition to 100 percent renewable energy by 2030, keep the water supply safe, and preserve public lands and wildlife habitats.

Another organization formed by young people concerned about climate change is iMatter (imatteryouth.org/campaigns). This group urges kids and teens to attend government meetings at the state and local level to push for changes such as reducing greenhouse gas emissions and stopping construction of new fossil fuel projects.

You, and I, and everyone can be heroes. And so can nature. It can help us. It has answers, if we just look hard enough. And listen.

Acknowledgments

I am forever grateful to my editor, Dana Carey, who gave this book the utmost attention, care, and love. Without her keen eye for detail and her ability to see the big picture, this story wouldn't be what it is. Thank you to Wendy Lamb for being our guiding star, and to Alyssa Eisner Henkin for always believing in my work and cheering me on, even when I doubt myself.

A round of applause to Celia Krampien for capturing the feel of the story with the vintage-postcard cover art and to designer Bob Bianchini for pulling the concept together. I am in awe of your talents since I can't draw a straight line. Thank you also to copy editors/comma queens Colleen Fellingham, Alison Kolani, Bess Schelper, and Kathleen Reed for your thoroughness and diligence with the manuscript.

I am greatly appreciative of the help I received from Gina LaLiberte at the Wisconsin Department of Natural Resources, Amanda Koch at the Wisconsin Division of Public Health, and Jackie Weber and Gregg Zink at

Integrated Lakes Management in Waukegan, Illinois. They never hesitated to answer my numerous questions and patiently explain scientific information. Thank you also to Mark O'Brien and Molly Pinta, who generously assisted with Zach's character.

As always, to Ben, Rachel, Sam, and Cassie: your unending support through all the ups and downs it takes to write a novel is valued more than you realize.

I took a leap of faith when I decided to have a beautiful, ancient lake and a river narrate part of this story. I feel strongly that nature has a voice, but we don't always hear it—or listen. Our actions affect the balance of all living things on our planet.

This life we have here is a gift. We need to cherish it.

About the Author

Michele Weber Hurwitz is the author of four other middle-grade novels, which have been on many state award lists and received several honors. She has lived in the Midwest for her entire life and has always loved spending time at Wisconsin's lakes. Sometimes she even hears one of them.

micheleweberhurwitz.com